Escape Mutation

A Journal of the Plague Years

William Essex

CLIMBING TREE BOOKS

First published 2020
under the title
Back to Nature.

Published 2021
under the title
Escape Mutation
by Climbing Tree Books Ltd.

ISBN 978-1-909172-97-5

Published by Climbing Tree Books Ltd, Falmouth, Cornwall

www.climbingtreebooks.net

Cover photo by Claire Wilson, LLE Photography

Cover design and typesetting by Grace Kennard

Escape Mutation is dedicated
to the memory of my friend
Andrew Waterworth.

Contents

Escape Mutation

A Journal of the Plague Years

Footnote to anybody reading this: *sorry for the scribble. I hope you can read my handwriting.*

Ignore the dates. This ridiculous fake-leather executive what-I-did-in-the-office diary is junk if I don't use it and I keep my Moleskines for serious writing.

It was Autumn when I started writing this, coming on to Winter. I started on Jan One because I didn't know how long I'd keep writing. Maybe fill the whole book. And it was Day One, near enough. Of Year One, call it.

*To you: hope it's legible. Started as a journal. ~~When I thought of doing it properly,~~ I found it easiest to write as a first draft, with the idea that I could tidy it up later. So it's a bit rough – sorry. ~~Don't skip the beginning; I want you to know me. I've been honest.~~

Hope you like it, reader of mine.

1st January

Looking out at a grey, grey, drizzly Summer-holiday morning. We used to come to beaches near here as children, on holiday, and this is the weather that brings those days back to me.

Happy childhood. Rain, wild seas, sand between my toes, picnics wrapped in beach-blankets and towels, under tarpaulins against the rain. We weren't hardy, or adventurous, but we'd go to the beach in just about any weather.

Years later, I think I was in my thirties, I remember a trip to Venice ~~with my first w.~~ We sat on a bench, under wide umbrellas, and read from a bag of books and magazines while rain sheeted down around us. That's what I remember of Venice.

It's not the rain nor the wild weather. The soul-experience was being out in it but sheltered against it, warm under a tarpaulin or under an umbrella, while the fresh, wild, exciting world happened around me.

~~This is the history of what happened. The plague years. But I want it to be my experience. My journal. It has to start with me.~~

I remember the sea, too; being thrown around by the breaking waves, diving under and over them, swimming out deeper, losing contact with the sand beneath my toes, diving down in a mask to look back up at the swirling waves.

And the sand. Building ramparts against the incoming tide. Dams across streams, plastic boats. The wind and the spray from the crests of the waves.

But those in-between moments – being there,

but being secure against it. In my mother's arms or just in the huddle of family. Those are the moments that settled into my soul. They define security for me.

2nd January

Perhaps that's it.

I was a natural at being locked down.

This works for me.

I'll get to all of it, but I want to remember how it was for me. ~~And then to write the book I came to write. My journal – these are the warm-up pages, but they're part of the story.~~

You'll have to wait. Or skip.

There's a recess in the rock, a shallow cave, not deep, clean, further down the path from here. It's dry. I've put an expendable garden chair there.

On a wild day, or when the mood takes me, I'll leave this warm, dry house, this comfortable leather armchair bought so cheaply from the charity shop in town, this fire of dry logs I cut myself, and sit out there with a mug of coffee and maybe a notebook. A pen.

I'll watch the weather. Listen to it as well. Stay dry.

"Are you the game-keeper?"

A woman asked me that once. Head-to-toe sky-blue waterproofs and walking poles.

"I live here."

"Oh."

She didn't get it.

"Down there. The house."

It's a small stone cottage built into the space in the rock left by an old dynamite works.

9

She still didn't get it.

The house isn't visible from the path just outside my cave, and this isn't the kind of place where you'd expect to find a house.

There was a mining industry here, a century ago, and they needed dynamite. They mixed it up in safe, remote places like this one. Then, where I live, the industry went away and the rich guy who owned the whole area built my small stone cottage. There's a story that he put a woman in it other than his wife. I don't know about that. She would have been comfortable.

"There's no gamekeeper here."

I said that to her, and there wasn't. Never was. Only ever just maintenance.

A gamekeeper would have found my vegetable garden and probably objected to it. Maintenance didn't look for vegetable gardens and didn't stray off the paths much. Not while I knew them, anyway.

They must have looked after the trees, so maybe I'm mistaken about that.

I grow spinach because I like spinach, carrots and potatoes. If we're talking about what I eat, I open tins, catch fish occasionally, nuts, nettles, shop things if I find anything I like still left on the shelves. I have traps and a gun, and they work, so I eat meat. But only occasionally. I'm not okay with that.

I thought she might say something else, but she went on up the path, and I watched her, and when she saw the house, she looked back. When she saw that I was watching her, she waved and I gave her a thumbs-up: yes, that house. Cottage.

3rd January

So we had our moment of human connection and that's why I still think of her occasionally. A relationship doesn't have to last more than a second to mean something. We had eye contact and then we waved and then we parted with all the potential between us left unopened. *I've forgotten her now.*

She was also probably the last uncomplicated human being I saw ~~before the~~. I didn't get out much, for obvious reasons. ~~But I don't think even if~~

Dogs used to find me in my cave, but walkers without dogs generally didn't notice me.

Some of them would stop to look at the cottage, but when they realised that it was occupied, they kept going. Some places look occupied and some don't, and mine doesn't.

It takes a moment even to notice that there's glass in the windows. I think that's because they're set quite deep in the stone so the sunlight doesn't reflect off them.

That's a defence. I think a lot about defending myself these days.

Walkers who looked for more than a moment would have seen that there was a fire lit inside. I kept a fire lit most days, still do, dry wood, because I like to tend to a fire. The cottage is colder inside than out at this time of year, and I like to think that I'm warming up the stones for the Winter.

The heating still works, but that's the past. For the future, I'm planning more towards relying on nature. If the fire does ever make smoke, because I've put on a damp log maybe, that smoke is usually pretty much the same colour as the woodland going up the slope behind.

You can see it, and the wavering heat in the air, but it's a corner-of-the-eye thing; it doesn't catch your attention.

Maybe you walk past and feel weird for a second, you know, like there's somebody there?

4th January

My cottage is a cottage, not a house. I looked up the difference.

A cottage has its upstairs windows poking out of the roof. My cottage could be part of the slope around it. Slate roof, green in places. Net to catch stuff falling down the back, covered in leaves. Fence too, for heavier debris, but you don't really see it.

Walls made of the local stone, front no higher than the cut-in of the path into the slope.

It's a wide path going all the way around the roughly 45-degree slope of the headland, half-way down the slope, so you can work out that the side of the path is about head-height. You could scramble up. But not easily.

Path wide enough for a car. But they never let cars up this far. Just maintenance came by occasionally. Phil in his yellow jacket, and Ken the same, side by side in the front of their near-silent electric utility vehicle, stopping to say hi if they saw me and for coffee if I offered, which I didn't very often after that first time (and neither did they). I don't think of myself as a recluse exactly, but I could never think what to say ~~and maybe they.~~

The raindrops on the windowpane merge into tiny little rivers and run down. I'm up in the bedroom looking down at the path. ~~I come up here sometimes and I don't remem~~

There's a lot of leaf-mouldy stuff on the path. Most of one season's layering? It's almost plain dirt but it doesn't take footprints very well. More like sponge. I think it's Autumn now. This year's leaves coming down as well. And of course there are no tyre tracks.

And now I'm back downstairs. I go up there sometimes and I don't remember why.

~~I never did like just opening the back door and going, although there's a big drain there and it's still clear. Kept a bit of civilised behaviour from the start.~~

The taps still work, although I've thought about what to do when they don't. ~~The septic tank is down by~~ This is a witness statement. My witness statement. If there'll ever be anybody to read it. I think I can leave out the septic tank.

I should carry this diary everywhere. If it wasn't so big. Just write down what happens. Happened.

The fire's lit and if I could summon up the energy, I'd eat something.

I get these days of just nothing. But I could leave some kind of record. I want to, more than memories.

The path falls away at the far side, almost like the mountain road in one of those films where the bus nearly goes over the edge.

And head-height is about right. I'd bang my head if I stood straight in my cave.

The car. Big explosion at the bottom. Always.

It's natural, not chiselled out.

~~Some days I'm just blank. I sit here and my thoughts go anywhere. Delayed reaction? Or just~~

~~not being able to think directly – shying off from it?~~

5th January

Starting again. ~~Delete previous entries? Childhood stuff later?~~
~~This is rough! Don't edit. Get it down!~~
My Journal of the Plague Years.

My cottage is well hidden on a public dog-walking path around a headland that's part of a big estate that now belongs to the National Trust. Look down from the path, and through the trees, you see water. Look up from the path, through the trees, and you might see the standing stones. But if you're looking up because your dog has bolted after a rabbit, you probably won't.

~~The weather comes down through the trees. It's not thick forest around me.~~

~~My cottage is not mentioned in the guide to the headland walk that is handed out at the gift shop. I never asked why not, because I didn't want to remind them.~~

~~This is too much information. I get too detailed sometimes.~~

~~But it's my record so it has to be about me.~~

I live here. I grow vegetables. I have traps, and they work, but I don't use them much. And a gun now. Same. Yesterday I scrambled down the bank and walked out onto the pontoon – it'll be stable for a while yet – and spent a while fishing. Once, a shoal of mackerel was boiling up the water right off the end of the pontoon and I didn't have my rod with me. I leave it down there now.

Spinners. Sometimes, I make an expedition

of it and dig for bait at low tide. Follow the path round and fish off the rocks on the other side of the headland.

Always catch something. It's a way to spend a day. Fishing. Barbecue. No disturbances.

And that's the weird part. You know how in stories, they set you up but they can't leave you alone? You get a situation that's safe, stable, interesting if it's fiction, a guy living a life. You want to stay in the first chapter?

But then they have to bring in the bad guy and the whole story is about making a mess of a situation that's happy-ever-after already, you know? Can't just leave it alone. Robinson Crusoe, safe on his island, building that stockade – I actually read the book, some of it – and then people turn up. The guy telling the story can't leave the guy alone to have his adventure.

~~I just want=~~
~~I just want=~~
~~Be careful what you wish for.~~
~~Enough deletions. Do this as "Morning Pages".~~
~~Just write. Let it come.~~
~~Nobody's going to~~

6th January

There were other books here when I moved in. A library of them. It's a holiday cottage and when I moved in there was a folder of instructions and local things to do on the table, and two clumps of beaten-up old paperbacks on top shelf, bottom shelf. *Robinson Crusoe, Treasure Island*, Daphne du Maurier, Rosamund Pilcher and that Dr Seuss about green eggs and ham.

15

PS: Receipts for the furniture! Instructions.

Three books by a name I didn't recognise with obvious romantic covers and a couple of thrillers by that newsreader. Some left behind by people staying and maybe a job-lot from a bookshelf in a back corridor of the big house. I guessed that, but I've seen the shelf since and I was right.

All this thinking time is doing me good. Mind in good shape.

I'm living a life in which there's no disturbance. An endless beginning, first chapters.

Originally, I took this place for nine months, although that's all gone now. Day One, I was doing that efficient thing of getting myself set up, not quite wound down from all the getting here from the previous place and arriving. I looked through the books for postcards, none, tidied them and pulled out *Robinson Crusoe*. Just curious. Flicked through, found the passage where he's building his stockade. Read most of that bit. Still open face-down by the bed. Maybe I'll go back to it.

Serendipity, finding that bit about the stockade.

I like the solitude. Which is lucky, considering. Ha ha.

The trees are loud in the wind – there's always enough of a wind – and on a ~~good~~ day when I've got my head together and I'm up for it, my work keeps me busy.

I'll get to that.

7th January

Write this as a record.

Every morning? Need structured days.

When the plague hit – no, that was the clever

part. The plague never "hit". It came in disguise.

When the plague reached me. Tell my version. Experience.

Busy day. The vegetable garden. I decided it was the day to do the replant with the biggest plants (fed up with waiting) but then I couldn't work out how to get them up the hill.

So I was out front on the path, not to make a mess inside, transferring my best seedlings from the trays, mugs, where they'd grown, into the big Tupperware box I'd found under the sink. Scrubbed out seriously in case it was used for cleaning. To use it just for the trip up.

~~Timeline. Need to explain the vegetable garden first. Go back two(?) weeks.~~

Two weeks before that, flashback. Chris and Ken came up the path on their wheels. I was out front then, too. They stopped. How was I settling in? I offered them coffee, and yes. But they had enough in their flask, so I just had to go fetch a mug. We stood out front.

They didn't know me and I didn't know them and we didn't have much in common to talk about so once we were set we stood around looking at the trees and not saying much. And then Chris asked me how I was getting on. I said – I remember this – that I felt like I was living off the grid. Ken asked me if the electrics were okay and Chris, I think he was joking, said about nature needing more maintenance than the built environment.

"Built environment." He was the younger of the two. I could have asked him about the course he'd done.

~~Electrics. Grid like an electric grid. Oh, I get it.~~
What I said was, I felt so off the grid that I

should be growing my own vegetables. Didn't mean it, just for ~~conversation, first thing that occurred to me,~~ emphasis, but of course they would have taken that seriously.

Growing vegetables wasn't something tenants in the cottage were expected to do, Chris told me.

Maybe a corner of the kitchen garden, behind the big house, Ken said, tentative, could be allocated next season if I was still here ~~(ha ha)~~, but it was all planted up this year, and…

No, it wasn't too late to plant a few seeds. Pots, maybe? Mind you, buying pots, or even paying to rent an allotment-space in the kitchen garden, was a bit more than maybe I had in mind?

"If we found a vegetable bed out here somewhere, nothing too big, maybe a few lettuces, we'd have to say something about it," said Chris.

"But we wouldn't go looking for a vegetable bed, would we?" said Ken.

"Wouldn't occur to us," said Chris.

We talked in a general way about rabbits and slugs and how bad an idea it was to use pesticides and other chemicals.

"If I had a vegetable bed, I'd never use chemicals," I told them.

We were liking each other, not quite laughing. I can't pinpoint when I'd stopped just playing along and started taking it seriously, but it was around about then.

"I'm partial to carrots, myself," said Chris.

"If we found a vegetable bed with carrots in it," said Ken, and then we did laugh.

I nearly spoiled the whole conversation by asking if I could borrow tools to dig a bed. But I didn't. ~~I'm thick like that sometimes, because I~~

~~can be awkward like that (no therapists in this new world), but I caught it before I blew it.~~

8th January

What I did was, I said good bye to them. But it stuck in my mind. Maybe a bit of it was, they'd be expecting me to do something. I did some research and realised that I actually could do it. Former city-dweller, fat old ex-everything, living off the grid and growing his own vegetables. It was possible. I did some research online.

After not much looking, because suddenly I was in a hurry, I found a more than averagely sunlit patch of flat ground at the top of the slope behind the house. Way away from any path or likely deviation off a path.

Then I went shopping in town.

This was two weeks (?) before Day One.

Hardware store and garden centre before supermarket. I spent more than I would have spent on renting an allotment (or buying a couple of big plastic troughs, obviously) and I bought everything. I was really into it and just kind of agreed with myself that I could be extravagant for once (and I didn't have to go back later for anything I missed ~~although I could have used seed trays~~).

First attempt, I dug deep and put down wire mesh, galvanised ~~(add: so unfit, etc., out of breath, mention it)~~. To stop moles and anything else fatter than a pencil that might try to dig under (add: had to stop and rest, etc.). Then put back the earth and sowed some seeds. I had bought the posts and the fruit netting, the staple gun, all that, but it was all still in the car and I decided none of it would be

19

necessary. I wanted to get on with writing the little labels.

I know what snail trails on bare earth look like now.

Fast forward two weeks to the second attempt.

This time, to get ready ~~for the second attempt at planting my vegetable garden~~, I brought some earth into the house and planted seeds in mugs, bowls and trays on or near the front windowsills. I ferried everything else up the slope and weighted it down under the green tarpaulin I'd bought.

Another ~~exhausting~~ tiring day, but I was beginning to get fit by then.

Then I waited for my seeds to hatch.

Germinate.

Get strong enough to fight off a snail.

9th January

That day when I noticed the absence of the riverboat and the walkers. Day One (or maybe it was Day Zero).

The day when I decided to take my biggest seedlings up to the vegetable bed and plant them.

Because I couldn't wait any longer.

Second Attempt Day.

Carrying a tray of earth and seedlings up a steep slope doesn't work. So I was out front with the Tupperware. See above.

I thought about the conversation I'd had with Chris and Ken approx. two weeks earlier ~~(emphasise timeline)~~, and that was when I realised that I hadn't seen them since then.

I ~~straightened up and (keep it real)~~ looked down the path, and no, no sign of them. Looking because I expected them. I usually saw them every other day or so, that time roughly, and surely somebody's law would dictate that they'd show up just as I was decanting vegetables?

We could have another conversation. I played it in my mind, how it would go.

Empty path. No walkers recently, either. And then the nagging thing that hadn't been nagging at me until that moment, if I'm honest, suddenly occurred to me.

No riverboat. Clear day, perfectly easy weather, no storms or turbulence – and no riverboat at all. Not once since I'd woken up.

Had it gone past yesterday? When did I last hear it?

Odd to remember it now. The riverboat's faint passing amplified commentary – "…coming up on the left you'll see…" roughly once an hour – had become a background to the day, like a church bell or traffic noise. ~~And occasionally seeing Chris and Ken go past.~~

I hadn't heard it at all that day, and – no, I couldn't remember the last time I'd heard it.

My thought was: odd time of year for a service. About the only thing I knew about the riverboat, because Chris or Ken had told me this, was that it would shut down for a couple of days of maintenance every end-of-season, before coming back as a ferry for the locals in Winter, without the commentary.

"You'll probably miss it," one of them~~, I think Chris,~~ had said. I hadn't even noticed its absence.

There's always a rational explanation.

The riverboat had broken down, obviously.

Quiet week in the walking season.

21

I decided that the peace and quiet was welcome. I should make the most of it.

10th January

I spent most of that day rigging up nets over the vegetable beds. I'd worked out a system. Snails were dangerous enemies, as rabbits would be, sheep also, and probably birds. But I was confident.

I went up the slope and put half my seedlings into my first bed and the other half into the second bed I'd dug next to it with enough ground for a path in between. The walled garden at the big house has beds with paths between, and I planned four beds. ~~Path in the middle each way. Simple cross, flag-like.~~

I stuck the original labels back into place. Then I made the frames I'd planned and not installed first time round. I cut the posts and nailed them together, then cut the fruit nets and used the staple gun to attach them to the posts. I dug down so that there was an overlap between the fruit nets and the wire mesh.

~~When I'd finished that, I had two planted-up vegetable beds with frames around them covered in fruit-net material. The frames were about a foot high off the ground. They were the sides, and now I had to make the lids.~~

~~Not lids. Framed nets. Frameworks of wood with fruit netting stretched across it and stapled into place.~~

~~I made those easily enough, and by the time I'd finished, I'd worked out how to fit them on securely. I made them same width and length as the frames overall, and then I nailed on extra~~

~~verticals, one at each side of each frame, one at each end, to stop them sliding sideways.~~

~~Somebody who knew what he was doing might have made something simpler, but I felt that I had maximum-security vegetable beds now. I was happy.~~

~~Too much information and muddled. Two beds dug, of four planned.~~ I enjoyed that day. This is a report.

11th January

In the evening I ate a can of beans with a spoon in my leather armchair and I remembered about the riverboat.

So I went online. Reluctantly, because I was feeling really tired and exercised and good about myself and I didn't want to puncture that.

I Google-searched the riverboat and came up with timetables and tourist-blah about the history of the river.

I didn't want to sign up for email alerts, or the newsletter, but I did click on the link in the news item about temporarily suspending service during the lockdown. Because it was dated this month, this year. ~~Two weeks ago, like everything else in this nightmare.~~

A lockdown? In Summer? No.

The link took me to a government briefing. Old-style, like every year. But not last Winter – two weeks ago. Odd.

I remember thinking: this year's wave of coronavirus has come early. The common worse-than-cold. But a Summer lockdown? That'll never fly.

I had my full-face masks and my gloves and the stockpile we all had by then: everything from tinned food to spare batteries, vitamin pills, generic aspirins, loo rolls and a diagnostic kit.

But – Summer?

Same old briefing. The new government crying wolf, I decided, talking it up just to get credit for taking it down.

"There's no immunity to this one," said the minister in answer to something, and I thought: yeah, yeah, you're new. "Aggressive mutation." Sure, right. Crying wolf. I gave him marks for coming across as sincere. Tame word, "variant".

Usual questions. Pretty much what you'd expect from journalists who'd done the pandemic story several years running. Nobody questioned the early lockdown either, which surprised me until I realised: they're just going through the motions.

I watched it all. Then I looked for a more recent briefing, but when I couldn't immediately find one, I shut down the laptop. Probably irritated with myself for losing so much time to TV.

I washed out the can and set it aside. I had some idea back then that I could use cans for something, if only I could work out what. So I kept them. Possibly bird-scarers (labels off) like you used to see old CDs and DVDs? Even just the ring-pull tops strung along a line.

I have a stack of cans out back. I'm old enough to remember two cans and a length of string taut between them. Early telephone. Remember that, but not the name of the boy I played with. What happened to him? Johnny Dee? Or did Mum just abbrev. his surname beginning with D?

I remember looking out of the kitchen window

at the backyard – the details of the cottage called it The Well: whitewashed space big enough for my tools, et cetera, (cans) shaded by a net above that needs to be cleared of the weight of leaf-mould regularly. There's a light out there, in its own little cage, switch in the kitchen, and I mentioned the big drain in the middle.

I remember looking out and thinking: pandemic come early this year. Lockdown. I'm off the grid. Well out of it.

I went back and stoked up the fire. I was still drinking back then and I had a little whisky left.

12th January

But that was an uneasy night.

If there is anybody reading this, you should know that I'm not stupid. The difficult thing is remembering how it really was. How it was before hindsight kicked in. And I had no reason to imagine, or guess, or work it out, or whatever you think I might have done about it.

Maybe I did ~~know without knowing~~ work it out. That was an uneasy night.

I woke up.

I must have slept – you know how you think this, after a sleepless night? – I must have slept because I woke up, I must have been asleep to wake up.

Daylight. I stared at the ceiling.

They didn't explain the R-number.

I checked the time.

I think that was the last time I ever needed to know the time – beyond day or night, morning or afternoon, hungry or okay – and sure enough, I had slept late.

Which meant that shops would be open in town. People would be about.

It was – Monday? Yes. A weekday.

They didn't explain the R-number.

"There's no immunity to this one."

A Summer lockdown.

Aggressive mutation.

FOR THE RECORD. These from the internet:

"Covid-19 has provoked more articles about how this isn't the planet getting its own back, than articles about how this is the planet getting its own back. We're so concerned to refute the notion that this is Gaia's revenge that you'd almost think we're worried that it might be."

"The virus does its thing, and our response has been to turn off everything we do to harm the planet."

"Imagine that this is a chance to re-run the history of the second half of the twentieth century, but without the toxic fluorocarbons, CFCs, the pesticides, all the science-improves-on-nature, and with videoconferencing and 3D printing."

Re-run further back than the twentieth century, maybe?

FOR THE RECORD. All quotes above are transcribed from blog posts I found dated around the beginning of the first wave.

Paradise Regained – another book title. I'm thinking in book titles.

Return to the Garden of Eden?

…Alone?

~~Observation: the word "Gaia" is okay to~~

mention in a way that "God" isn't. Proofs of the existence of Gaia? Underfoot? How do religions form? So much is newly unknown now. Who's alive? How did this happen? We're okay with the idea of a sentient planet, or was Gaia just every living thing working like clockwork? working in harmony?

13th January

I got out of bed and I went downstairs and I walked outside. Bare feet. I had actual pyjamas back then. Made footprints. The breeze was rustling through the trees. Sunlight was slanting through the leaves. At the bottom of the slope I could see the water glittering.

There's something about that time of year. It's in the guidebook. Middle of the Summer, the early sunlight hits one of the standing stones through the others. Month later, for a short while, it shines right up the creek.

There was no human sound. I remember that moment. Just sunshine, aslant, and the sound of the breeze.

I stood in a patch of sunlight and felt myself warmed.

No R number.

No numbers at all.

So far as I could remember, it had all been about DNA and molecules and vectors and how this bit hooks on to that bit and the immune system doesn't recognise – whatever.

How many dead? Somebody had asked.

Some version of a politician response.

Let's see if I remember it. "They were still

collating the numbers because they'd updated
their counting methodology and he was concerned
to make sure that, something, and later he'd be
releasing updated numbers, something, accuracy,
yada, methodology, blah, always made it very clear,
something, reluctant to put out numbers that he
might have to update, yada yada, something, keep
on talking until they forget the question, blah
blah, timed out, next question." (Something like
that. But it reads like generic politician made-up
stuff = cheap. Stick to what you remember and
keep it real.)

He avoided the question.

Why hadn't I picked up on that while I was
watching it?

Maybe I had. Sleepless night.

Aggressive mutation.

I went back inside

I went into the backpack I hadn't unpacked
and took out my most comfortable facemask and
a pair of gloves.

14th January

I locked up the house and walked back to the
beginning of the path where there was a metal
gate before a cattle grid and a parking area. Also a
noticeboard on a post about byelaws and lighting
fires and an honesty box that I once found Chris
and Ken emptying – people are honest. On another
post, my metal post-box – empty. I'm far enough
off the grid not to get discount vouchers for take-
out pizzas. That far off the grid. Big distance once.
[Also not far away, my septic tank. It hasn't needed
emptying yet. I don't know how I would know if it

did. I don't think about it.]

No other cars. A drift of aerial seeds and twigs caught on my windscreen wipers. Nobody could accuse me of cleaning that car too regularly. I reconnected the battery, checked the tyres and used the jack to remove the blocks and let the car back down onto its wheels.

The battery was dead, but started first time when I connected the charger unit that I kept under a blanket in the back.

I put the charger unit on the passenger seat to take back into the house and recharge.

Then I drove back down the long, narrow access road – path – to the grounds of the big house. Nothing had been up here for a while. I had to stop twice to clear fallen branches. On the way back I'd pick them up for firewood.

The gift shop was closed. I turned on the radio to check what day it was.

I haven't carried a phone since they failed to cancel the surveillance thing a second time and nobody objected.

Maintenance was closed. No sign of either of them.

The music just kept on playing. I tried for another station, but twisting the dial just got me white noise or once or twice music. I left it.

Weekday. Yes. I was sure. There were three cars in the big-house public car park. No people that I could see.

I drove through and out onto the road.

No traffic. No surprise. We were in a Summer lockdown. I wasn't panicking yet.

I drove into town.

15th January

My work. I'm in the funeral business. Burial. I drive the backhoe. Self-taught.

When I got back to the cottage on that first day, Day One or Day Two or whatever it was, I set the battery charger to charge, then I looked around at the empty space where I would be spending the rest of the day.

My rental cottage: the cheap armchair, the table, the fireplace, the trays and the mugs. The books.

And then I went for a walk.

I walked round the headland to the bench at the furthest point, where there's an uninterrupted view of the wide-open sea and the docks on the right.

All the nature and all the peace and all the calm that you can get. All the sky and all the horizon and all of the nature.

Grass. The bench. The breeze. The clean air.

I took my mask off and my gloves off. I took a deep, deep breath, like drinking cold water on a hot day.

I sat down on the bench and watched nothing happen. No walkers.

No ships, no smaller craft, nothing.

"What the fuck, T.H.?" I said out loud

The bench has a brass plate. The guy died last year, much loved, missed, his initials, and I speak to him occasionally. Not because I'm religious or I think he's standing over me, I don't know why, but out of respect for the emotion maybe, the people missing him who paid to put a brass plate here. T.H. A man who died at eighty-four and left behind generations of people who missed him enough to pay for a brass plate. Respect for all that. Eighty-four years. Wife, children, grandchildren.

Space for another name on the brass plate.

Birdsong. The birds were okay.

The wind was off the sea. Light cloud. Silence.

"Oh, fuck, T.H.," I said.

I remember that I tried to work out, in a way that felt mathematical, logical, step-by-step and above all self-controlled, what I should be seeing and hearing right at that moment.

There would be one or two ships moving in our out and a lot of tiny white sails going around the buoy in the middle.

But it was okay that there weren't. Sometimes there weren't ships and yachts racing.

There would be noise. But.

There would be people, tiny in the distance. But.

All that broke down. It wasn't there any more.

There was nature. Just nature. Fresh and implacable.

In the town behind me, I thought of it as my home town now, where the supermarket was, there had been nobody. All the shops closed. No traffic. Not a single person. Nothing.

The air had not been clean.

I hadn't explored. I'd started to drive the familiar route at first, around town and to the supermarket, but did a sudden U-turn on Minchin Street and come straight back.

Best way to describe it – with hindsight, now – is: I was pacing myself into the knowledge, letting it in bit by bit so that I didn't just scream and panic and go racing back into town to find somebody, anybody, and just hold them close to me. Until–

Oh, fuck, T.H.

We'd had the first coronavirus, the second wave, the year after that, the Winter Measures that everybody just accepted, and then the whole thing with the "Cull" – the bad year.

People make humour out of anything. Give it a name at least. Rona. The Cull.

Rona mutating. Worse every year.

I sat on that bench and I did not panic.

16th January

We do a good funeral. Mass graves, they have to be, but there's still gasoline.

Burial. But it is a funeral. We stand and watch. And then I get back in the cab and push the earth back over them.

I found the first living person when I drove back into town a day after Day ~~One Two~~ Whatever. All wrapped up, windows of the car closed. No aircon but.

Such a relief.

I cried and he started crying. *She?

We stood at opposite ends of the street, me beside my car, and cried at each other. He was wearing a diving mask with most of a sheet wrapped round his head. I had my facemask and a pair of ~~old-fashioned driving goggles. No. Still the safety glasses~~ back then.

The smell was bad.

We were shouting to each other and another man heard us. He came. *She came?

The burials were my idea. I'd driven past the backhoe and a dumper truck and a forklift left out in the open at the builder's yard. I shouted that I'd be back. We kept our distance from each other and we didn't exchange much information. We were too scared of everything. In shock.

But I'm getting this out of order. ~~Again.~~

Three of us at first, eventually eight of us at most. Forklift, backhoe, dumper truck, hatchback.

We couldn't work together. We could never get together. We knew that from the start.

We kept our distance from each other and boy, we were well-wrapped. Call it anti-social distancing.

I don't think we're immune. I think we're the loners.

We wrap up against each other, against the bodies, the weather, anything on the air. Outdoor gear, big puffy jackets, tarpaulins like ponchos, ski masks, visors.

I think some of us ~~were~~ are women. Think. Thought. Thought even then. ~~I didn't see you there.~~ *You tell me!*

We were burying the dead because leaving them would be worse. And I think just slightly because it's the only thing we can justify doing together. I caught the habit of wrapping up from them.

We look more like mummies than zombies, but you don't have to see too many of the dead before you want an airtight suit like in *Contagion* or one of those other movies. Wrapping up feels like the next best thing.

And we shout to each other. There's a sign language to go with that, for when I'm behind the engine-noise of the backhoe.

One of them might be Chris. But I don't think so. *Tell me when you get to this bit. I want to talk to you about it.*

I sat on that headland for two hours at least, on that first morning of the end of the world, and nobody came.

No dog snuffling at my boots and jumping up.

No walker shouting the dog's name and being ignored.

No traffic on the sea, no sound from the docks and no movement that I could see in the streets and the terraces behind the docks.

I'm going to go on being honest. I must. No point otherwise.

My experience. How it was for me.

Just the birds and the wind, that day. Beauty. Call it an omen?

*Hope you liked the beginning.

17ᵗʰ January

I went back because I was lonely. ~~Desperate to be wrong.~~

Don't call it lonely. A word too ordinary. If I was right, then everybody else was dead. I was desperate to be wrong. But it took me a day to nerve myself to go back and prove it either way.

Online, I found the beginning and the updates until the news stopped. The panic, call it. But the rest of the internet was still happily trying to sell me stuff.

The social media was awful. We chew each other's legs off in a trap. Closest I came to thinking – we deserve this.

The radio gave me music.

I managed to convince myself that none of that was conclusive. That this was just an unusually disruptive outbreak of coronavirus and we'd be back to normal after the authorities or the emergency services or whatever got back in control. ~~I was in an altered state. Or just crazy.~~

Helicopters come flying in like what was that film?

Not dreams exactly. Scenes from the old world flaking off.

Vivid dreams. Queues of people.

It was my idea to do it one street at a time and start by going from house to house and opening or smashing all the windows. Get the air in. We weren't going to need the houses again.

We used sledgehammers.

I got up from the bench and walked back to the cottage. There would be tools and equipment in the maintenance sheds behind the big house. I could put an extra chain on the gate that stopped cars coming any further. If I was wrong, they'd know it was me. What's a padlock between friends, if the world's still alive?

And pry-bars.

Walking back to the cottage, I selected a tree. Walking further than the cottage, I selected another tree. Big trees. Not the biggest, but by the standards of my woods, bulky.

The weirdest part is that I picked those trees before I knew what I was going to do with them. Not exactly unconscious, but I was planning without telling myself about it. Altered state. Can't explain it.

I took my gardening tools up to my vegetable garden and dug another bed, three of four. I didn't think about concealment. I'd get to planting it, and putting up nets and fencing, some other time.

When I'd finished, I sat up there, my back to one of the stones, for felt like an hour.

~~Altered state. Call it During Traumatic Stress Disorder, call it that. DTSD. Traumatic Stress.~~

I wanted to think but I didn't want to think.

I went back down to the cottage and found the instruction manual for the generator. I still had electricity, and fuel, and I knew how to work the generator, but being practical, planning ahead, is a distraction in itself. Keep it busy. I opened up my laptop. There was still an internet. But staring at the screen was too static. I locked the front and back doors, all the windows, and lit the fire.

Then I got really angry.

18th January

Ran to the car like I was going to punish it. I drove the car down to the maintenance sheds. Fast. I took the axe with me that I use for chopping logs, and the spike I use for splitting them. It was easier than I had expected to break in. I made a circuit of the big house ~~(Thinking ahead like picking the trees?)~~ – still no sign of anybody, not even in the private section where the family live, not going to think about that now – and the car park – ditto – before I loaded up.

I left the car in its usual spot back at the gate – I'd thought this through – and used the wheelbarrow – the looted wheelbarrow – to carry my looted tools up to the cottage.

Then I spent whatever was left of that day felling the two trees I'd selected. ~~I think it was that day.~~ Bringing them down on the path. It was frightening work. I knew what I was doing, pretty much, but I wasn't sure how firm the ground was. I did some digging, and got a small avalanche that took me with it. Not enough to block the path, so I had to keep going. I dug up-slope next, all the while afraid that the roots would come whipping up out of the ground quickly enough to hit me.

I cut at roots, ~~cut~~ sever one and step back, sever another and step back. The first tree started to go. I needn't have worried quite so much. The ground shifted ~~too slightly to notice~~, I jumped back out of the way, and the tree would have caught me if it had gone straight down – but there was noise. It moved, creaked, and then rested.

I went to the second tree. By then, I'd worked out that if it didn't go down immediately, the weather would finish it off eventually. I'd just have to avoid the path.

The first tree came down. Suddenly. A creak like a rusty hinge opening, then a crash and a kind of 'shush!' as the branches hit the ground, then frightened birds, then silence.

The path was blocked well enough to stop anybody approaching the cottage without making enough noise to warn me. I thought! There was a crater in the slope, but nothing you could scramble up too easily.

~~Almost a shelter, with the mass of root.~~

I brought down the second tree same way, dancing away from it when it even looked like it was ready to go, not waiting too long, took the chainsaw to the bigger branches, and took a can of lager to my cave. I sat there thinking about recycling. I felt secure.

Don't ask. Yes, there was one. Chainsaw. Big petrol thing. Scared me, honestly. Not the time to learn how to use it.

19th January

I'd shut myself in, of course, blocked the path before and after the cottage, but that was a small price to pay for sleeping at night. I took my time over finding a secret route out, down and round, and I told myself I wouldn't let it get worn into a path.

~~I don't know what I was afraid of. But~~

For the vegetable beds, I just went straight up. You have to live here to know where to climb up off the path.

About once a week, less often now, I go back down and use the backhoe to dig. The park by the river has soft ground. In a day, I can dig enough space for – I don't count. I'll need to find a new park soon.

For burial, after the fire, I just push the earth back over them.

~~Afraid of the wrapped people.~~

The only fight I ever saw was at the supermarket, two wrapped people, but I'd come in the forklift with a small skip out front and a dead person's shotgun in my free hand, so I didn't get much trouble.

I think they're happy to have me burying the dead. They don't volunteer. We don't speak. I leave the backhoe blocking the road when I drive home. I ~~think~~ know they know where I am, but they also know that I've got at least one firearm.

We're not enemies. Nobody I know. Pretty sure I recognise one or two of them from before. We don't acknowledge each other, either.

I have treasures, a few of them. One or two pieces of jewellery that I saw, as I was carrying their owners out into the street, and some practical things. No crime. I broke into a couple of shops. The supermarket's run out of most things now.

We've settled into the new life now, the survivors. No need to go into town any more. My vegetables are growing, and I've eaten meat that I killed myself – not again, but I know I can do it. The animals have lost the habit of hiding from us. They're tame, almost. They're not crowded out by the human race.

I found a couple of fishing rods the other day, new ones. They're down by the river.

20th January

Last night I came out and looked at the sky. It's bigger than it's ever been, and so much deeper. So many stars. I sat out on the bench at the open end of the headland, under the dome of the heavens. I can see so far.

The car still has a little petrol left in it, and that's for town or the big house, but I've found a bicycle. The burial work is mostly over, nobody comes, so it's just occasional foraging for something I think I need – or for whatever I might find when I'm in that mood.

I spend my evenings learning everything. The internet's a survivor so far. I can't even work out how the electricity's still alive, let alone Google. But it's all there. Maybe there's some kind of failsafe back-up that kicked in, or they were further along with self-sustaining AI than anybody knew. Skynet, maybe, after the nuclear fire. Do I explain film references?

I think this about the internet. One bad Winter, and who's going to be climbing the telegraph poles? For a while I thought there were people, enough people to keep the electrics running, all safe in their stockade somewhere but still not able to come and rescue us yet. I don't think that any more. Fossil fuels warmed up the Winters, didn't they? One Bad Winter and it's coming. Winter is coming.

So I read anything I can find online about cooking and farming and growing vegetables, trapping animals, natural remedies, what you can eat in nature and what you can't – anything I can find. I'm living through the half-life of knowledge, and I want to get as much of it into my head before it all goes dark. I know how to make fire (and I did it once, so I know I know how to make fire), lance a boil, scavenge enough to eat from a patch of woodland, make a lobster pot, mend socks, cauterise a wound, set a broken bone, a lot of things, some more likely to be useful than others.

Cure animal skins to make clothes. I sledge-hammered the windows of a bookstore. Struck me that if the electricity goes, nothing to watch.

Deliver a baby. Smoke fish.

How to learn? I loaded up the reference section.

I picked a street and then I went from house to house, opening the windows. The bodies are becoming less human now so not so bad. Such clear skies.

Then I bring them out. I didn't work every day and I don't suppose it really matters. Too difficult or too heavy, I left them. Leave them.

I haven't gone anywhere near the hospital. That can wait.

Sleep now.

21st January

Found a jigsaw in the cupboard. Big one, thousand pieces. Gave me something to do with the dining table. I cleared the chairs out of the way, swept off the curled-up leaflets like ancient history, ~~local attractions of a dead civilisation,~~ and the dust and dragged the table over to the window to get some light on it. Then I tipped out the pieces and started to look for edges.

Just the bottom half of the box so no clue as to the picture. There's a lot of sky so far, and I found the two sky-coloured corners. I think it's a painting not a photograph. Something dark. Possibly a lot of trees.

How long before I put it away again? Ever?

The internet went off. The lights failed. Been on the generator when I need it for a while now. I'm starting not to need it. The fireplace is where I can cook if I want hot. Using the insides of the oven and empty cans, stones either side to make a barbecue. Works okay but I eat cold mostly. Foraging, vegetables.

Check the traps.

22nd January

Broke into the big house a few days ago. Thought about living in it for a while then just curious – maybe food in there. No harm, no foul. Nobody to object. Unless.

I drove round it, close in (on the gravel), and then around the grounds. I was looking for signs of people who might have been living there all along, the family I mean, or people who had moved in already. Plague people, loners, avoiding each other.

I think the way through this is to avoid confrontations or getting into people's territory.

Then I parked round the back, close up to the wall, down by the side of that bit jutting out, with the steps curving down either side.

Don't know why the heck I was hiding the car. I locked it.

Backed in. Empty car. Indoor foraging.

Got the worst part out of the way first. The beds were disturbed in the children's rooms, but they'd all got together in the parents' big bed for the end. Nobody else. Couple of rooms obviously lived in, servants or butlers or whatever, but long gone. The air had that smell to it, but gently now.

I left windows open.

We're all going back to nature, aren't we?

And I don't know if this is crazy but I had the sense they would have wanted that.

Maybe my Emotional Self is hearing from ghosts.

Decided not to live there.

Make it my place to find things, safe from town.

FOR THE RECORD. These also copied down from way back.

"Despite all the committees ranged against it, the government scientific advisers, the daily briefings, the slide shows and the statistics, the whole not-travelling circus, the inconvenient truth is that Covid-19 isn't losing this fight."

"We're going to be infectious to each other for a while yet. But we need to get back to work. That, I think, qualifies as a new normal."

"How do we devise a society – not an economy, a society – in which we can obtain what we need by co-operating with people whose very presence may be dangerous to us? By squabbling over whether or not the government should have advised us to wear facemasks? I don't think so."

"The government was too slow to impose the lockdown, and we're outraged about that, but it is now prioritising The Economy over The Virus – and the shops are open again! Yippee! We're all gonna buy!"

23rd January

I broke in by breaking a pane of glass in the not very secure wooden door round the back where I parked the car, right in the corner under the thingy. Balustrade? Word should mean that.

So well hidden I didn't see there was a door as well as windows until I'd parked.

After I broke the glass – door was unlocked.

Coats and hats and gumboots inside, and in the next room, shelves, machines, laundry hanging from a kind of pulley thing from the ceiling and a big dog basket next to an old Aga. Not lit; cold. Flagstones. ~~I'm not describing this very well.~~

It was a kitchen.

But – servants' kitchen? Original kitchen?

A utility old kitchen no longer used except for gumboots and laundry.

Never saw any dogs.

In the big rooms up from there, carpets and sofas and pictures on the walls. Fireplaces. There was a big NEW family kitchen with light and places to sit up and have breakfast. It was a very DESIGNER kitchen out of a magazine, light and new.

Stone floors in the main corridors?

Flagstones. Front entrance. Tiled kitchen floor. Most of inside the house, and upstairs, planks – floorboards. Wood echoes. Rugs.

The stairs very worn, wide, with generations of people going up the wide part and turning left or right under the big picture. Turned my head and there was a gallery round the stairwell. About an acre of skylight above. Kill the house when that breaks. So many pictures, overlay of people actually living there, bits and pieces and possessions. Not describing this very well.

That echo of floorboard corridors. Creaks. Latched doors to the bedrooms at the back, clanky bathrooms. Proper bedrooms at the front, proper door-handles. Solid doors.

The family, dead and gone. Dead and still there. By the time they got it, no help to come? All together in the big bed (like a still life, I thought later – there were paintings of dead game birds and vegetables as well as people and landscapes).

I decided not to live there. My job was to open the windows, give them some air.

24th January

In the kitchen, the new expensive kitchen, there was a big fridge-freezer still working although my electricity in the cottage had gone off by then. The food inside was still good. Eggs. They hadn't cared so much about clearing the breakfast bar and the worksurfaces towards the end. I did it for them, washed up. Then I made myself a mug of black coffee using their machine, poured the spoiled milk down the sink, and sat at the breakfast bar. There were clip-frames on the walls of family photographs. Running water.

I thought that I should think about them, or mark their passing, or make some kind of gesture. I knew their names.

I found this diary in a drawer of the desk in the big room.

With it there were letters, not personal. Financial reports and certificates. School reports, receipts. I found out birth dates and ages and was beginning to look through the records of their wealth when it occurred to me that I could still respect their privacy. Do that for them.

I thought about setting the house on fire. A funeral pyre like we had been doing in town. I thought about bringing their bodies out and burning them in the garden. I decided to leave the house as it was, with the windows open, and let them go slowly back to nature. They were together already.

I thought about loading up the car and taking all their food back to my cottage. I did take some of it, and the .22 rifle I found, and the shotgun, but I decided to leave everything for another day.

My favourite tool, my weapon of choice, would be a hammer or a hatchet.

Used a hammer and chisel to open the lockbox. The gun cabinet. Then I thought to look in all the other drawers of the desk and found the keys to finish the job. ~~Searched everything locked.~~

I think that jigsaw is a picture of a forest. Do some more of it before the light goes.

25th January

Wet day. Fire lit. Kettle boiling. Time to start my ~~autobiography family history Journal Story My Story of the Plague Years (working title)~~ serious work.

I shall start it here.

Wet days inspire me. I've got a rhythm established of writing in this book. Not to be superstitious, but let's not break that rhythm. Write it rough here and then tidy it up for the designated notebook. Then the laptop, for the final digital draft.

If digital is a thing now.

I bought these notebooks, these pens – these A5 light-blue hardback Moleskines and these Pilot G-Tec-C4 gel pens, and I set them out on this dining table and so far I've done nothing with them except write occasional notes in one and move them all to the shelf.

But today – today, I woke up with the right words to get started in my head. *Even if nobody reads this except you, I shall write it. Leave it lying around (Claudius?). ~~For posterity, ha ha.~~*

Opening sentence. I came here because I haven't been here for fifty years. ~~Take in: memory from 1st January. Clarify: We used to come here as children on holiday. To come to beaches on the North Coast, to a beach on the North. Not "here".~~

I came here because I haven't been here for

fifty years and I needed somewhere ~~secure~~ remote but secure to recuperate. ~~And I'd been lying there remembering and it hurt.~~ In the first week away from the hospital, I knew I had to get away from all the reminders. So I booked myself an out-of-season holiday cottage ~~(not this one, or is that obvious?)~~ for a fortnight, ~~near there (family holidays of childhood, write more, say where, not far off but),~~ packed up the car like I was never coming back, closed up the house, and drove down.

I felt weak. I tired easily. But I needed to be away.

Suza. Suza. Eddie. Suza.

Suza. And me. And little Eddie. Not Edward. I'll tell you about the book of names, and how long it took, and then we were sure, and then he could never have had any other name. Eddie. She was Suzanne – but Suza.

26th January

It was a motorway journey rather than that half-remembered interminable run through the towns and hedges of my childhood, but I'd planned for that. I made stops along the way, detours to place-names I remembered and wanted to see again, and by doing that, I brought back something of the past.

The long, slow journey back into myself, recreated in the driving seat of a modern city hatchback rather than the back seat of an old Volvo. ~~Too cute. Kill your darlings.~~

And I suppose those first five days of my rented fortnight ~~in the deep past~~ did give me clarity on what I needed to do next with my life.

I slept for the first day. I was barely conscious for the run to the supermarket to get provisions, then I collapsed straight back into bed.

On the second day, I found the beach. Smaller than I remembered. Less remote.

I sat against the familiar curve of a familiar rock and summoned up ghosts.

I watched myself playing in the waves, and gradually, as I remembered, those waves became large again, some my height, some bigger than me, and I sat there in the respite from the wind almost hearing my mother's voice. "Be careful!"

That thing with the people you love. You can't help but state the obvious. "Stay safe!" "Be careful!" "Don't fall over!" As if.

"Don't catch the plague!"

I tried to find the pub. The building was there – again, smaller – but it wasn't the pub as I remembered it. The pub that had sold ice creams after the beach – we'd sat outside to eat them and my parents had raised glasses to each other.

Their eye contact. Their shared life. I forget the names of the ice creams. Mivvi?

And then on the third day, I'd–

On the third day, I understood that I hadn't driven all this way, packed up everything, just to spend two weeks wandering around the remembered places.

By lunchtime on the third day, I understood what I had to do.

By the evening, I'd collected details, spoken to people, made appointments to view, resigned my old life.

Scattered the ashes.

Scattered the ashes into the wind and decided

resolved to move on with my life.

27th January

Is "hope" the right word?

There was almost a thrill to it. Something was actually happening for once.

I've thought about this a lot. We talked about it. Those early days of the first lockdown in the city. The empty streets. Suza found the music for it. The end of the world. Played that track all the time. We were feeling fine.

Not hope. You come out of the cinema and you've got to wake up from whatever it was. We were in this ~~sudden total~~ collapse and we kept on having moments when we weren't waking up from it. Always time to wake up ~~but it was real.~~ and finding that we were awake already. Not a good nor bad feeling just strange to pin down. We talked about it.

Dread? Too alive for dread.

Bad news but without the deadening sense of "Oh no, more bad news." Alive bad news.

How does suspension of disbelief work if the unbelievable is real? The incredible? Suspension of credibility.

That was the beginning.

28th January

I was around when "twenty-four-hour rolling news" was introduced, and what they didn't say was, we'll be playing the same reports every fifteen minutes until the end of time. It will be BORING.

Back then, I had television ("smart") as well as

the internet with all the trimmings and two digital radios. Analog in the bathroom. I wasn't cut off from anything. I was film-literate. I remember saying to Suza: for this, we're gonna need a bigger television.

But the deadly global pandemic virus turned out to be boring.

(Insert: plague crept up on us, etc.)

A lot of news talked about how bad it would have been if governments had done nothing. If nobody had imposed a lockdown. Then a lot about how they should have locked us down earlier, change the rules with more notice, all that. We found out how bad it would have been if they'd done nothing, because that's how bad it was when governments tried to reimpose everything – second year, remember? – and nobody took any notice everybody argued.

Remember the thing in the US about freedom? Shooting each other over mask-wearing?

I used to travel a lot. Crazy when you think about it.

A huge metal flying torpedo with wings carries hundreds of people to a remote location where they've got no immunity. Where they don't belong.

At the same time, another big metal torpedo carries the same number of different people to where the first lot started.

Where they've got no immunity.

Group A gets sick with B's germs. Group B gets sick with A's germs.

And then they go back home.

Taking their new germs with them.

Pity you couldn't check your immunity into left-luggage before you left.

For the next guy to use.

No wonder the airlines failed.

29th January

Before all that, first time with the virus, at the very beginning, even before the fear and horror that had come before the ~~what word? = complacency. Wrong word. The~~ getting used to having it around. *Before politicians found they couldn't fix it so made it our problem.*

~~I've thought about this a lot. Said this!~~

That first time, I'd had an almost-guilty-pleasure feeling that the world was changing. Something was happening. Remember that so strongly.

Don't feel good about it ~~(but this is a record and being honest)~~, but nothing had sunk in that early. No death numbers on the TV every day. ~~Didn't know anybody who~~

Getting worse every year.

~~Now, this year, today, timeline, the edge-of-consciousness worst case that hadn't happened yet back then = has happened.~~

~~And I'm living in a remote cottage that I took for a minimum nine months that would run over the winter.~~

~~Had I known? How long had I known?~~

Chapter Two: When I Met Her. This is the "before" picture of the relationship. Before I met Suza and we had Little Eddie. Who both died in the ~~so-called fucking~~ Cull. ~~I can't call it that.~~

Even with present love, we should be able to ~~talk~~ speak of past love.

This is the history. The death of my wife and child, but also now the collapse of ~~liberal democracy~~

~~The West Western~~ Human Civilisation.

Chapter Two starts with that first lockdown.

Adventure? We had a full fridge, pasta, bread, loo rolls and cash. Roughly £200 in folding money, between us, the same-ish in each of our current accounts. She had some savings accessible via online banking and I had a small-to-not-very-rich portfolio of investments that were crashing further every day.

I think we did start with it being an adventure. ~~No deaths yet, no harm; back then it was the novelty of staying home. I grieved for that money = inherited money, rich uncle, check my family name; yes, that family = and she teased me. "Come on, you never touch it." / "But it's security." Ha ha.~~

FOR THE RECORD. One more scribbled-down quote from a blog post. Back at the beginning, I really wanted to keep a record of how it was.

"This is real. Like everybody else, I want it to end. But – what better display of human nature could there be than all the 'Minister, could you tell us your plan to get everything back to normal?' questions that now dominate the daily briefing? File those under: Fate, tempting."

30th January

"We've passed the first test," she'd say.

That was her joke. The first test was being somewhere safe with adequate supplies when the thing kicked off. This wasn't a zombie apocalypse but we'd passed that test. ~~We aren't going to die in the first episode, I remember her telling me. As if it was~~

~~Neither of us took it seriously at first.~~

I remember on that first morning, I sat out on the front step and drank tea and felt more alive than I had in a long time.

She came and joined me.

We looked up the silent mews to the street that should have been full of traffic and heard the city's idea of silence.

"Wow," she said.

We had two facemasks bought from a DIY store and never used – I never did sand that door – and a bottle of hand-sanitiser left over from her volunteering at a homeless shelter. Later, we made our own facemasks.

That morning. In the city.

~~We weren't even taking the lockdown seriously.~~

Her pointing out that we could hear birdsong.

I thought: this is real.

Then I thought: we're safe. We have money and supplies.

I was so naïve back then.

~~We made~~

31st January

That was the opening scene of the reality we were in.

Suza pointing out that this was the first apocalypse in which it was still possible to order a take-away pizza.

~~She never took it seriously.~~

No cars, no traffic. The Jensens packing up and heading out to their place in the country. The family at the end catching on and doing the same. Big hurry to get out.

All those second-home people.

We almost had the mews to ourselves.

Deliveries. Social distance.

Getting into a new rhythm of the day.

The big one-piece-of-exercise walks down to the river. The social distancing by stepping off the pavement. Complicit smiles from like-minded people.

I remember social media about flu. Was flu more deadly than the virus? Was this some jumped-up flu bug to fill a slow-news week, or some exaggerated prospect of disaster to keep the talking heads busy now that the election was over, or the real unscripted thing?

There was an election, I remember.

Suza and I together in the mews, eating out front in the mornings with the sun, sometimes carrying the table across for the sun in the evening.

Those weeks when we hardly did anything and once or twice even missed our once-a-day walk. River, round the park, sometimes window-shopping.

The benches taped off.

This was a time to meditate, we agreed, her arm in mine.

To reflect, re-evaluate, take it slowly before returning to a more considered way of life.

~~I can't bear it.~~

~~We made plans.~~

1st February

I was somewhere between DREADING that it was real and HOPING that it was real and not wanting to take it too seriously.

Could this be real? Really?

I can almost forgive myself for the HOPING. ~~It was a strange time.~~ The death-count wasn't on the news yet. They hadn't begun the daily briefings.

So long ago now.

The first wave and that fresh, optimistic time in which we thought the little round coloured-in bug with the suckers was going to change the way we lived.

~~Remember the beach party in that ad for a fizzy drink?~~

Goodbye to globalisation and departure lounges; hello to the New Normal in which we all ate organic and the canals ran clear.

And then all those mindless efforts to get us back into the old normal when nothing had changed except the centre had run out of money.

Two-metre social distance. Then "one metre plus". All those slogans.

"Stay safe." Yeah, thanks.

The riots in the US. They had an election too.

Lockdowns ended, virus still out there.

Masks in shops. Arguments about masks.

Local lockdowns, local power.

Same old virus, second wave.

Then the change.

2nd February

Do I write this every day?

Not feeling so good today. Ate something. Not good.

~~Do I write about the change? When it became obvious undeniable that~~

~~Think about it tomorrow.~~

3rd February

That's *Green Eggs and Ham*? Seriously? Doctor Seuss?

Point being TO EAT the green eggs and ham?
~~I never read this to~~
~~We were never a Dr Seuss fam~~
~~He liked~~
Not the book I need to read right now.

I'm lying here, still with stomach cramps, head clear but feeling really weak, in a slew of random books grabbed from the shelf and twisted-up tangled sheets, restless night, restless day, reading a children's book about eating green eggs. And ham.

Menu recommendations for the apocalypse.

Bed all yesterday.

Suza would have clicked right into this. Water, fruit tea. Getting me up. Open windows, fresh sheets.

"It's just Man Flu!" she would have said by now and I would have protested.

"Darling, it's food poisoning!"

~~Never called her darling. Memory plays tricks simplifies tells a story fakes~~

~~I can see the expression on her face, that minute little shake of the head and the smile from close-up as she did whatever to the pillow and me reaching up~~

~~Thought: how do I clean my teeth without toothpaste?~~

Getting thinner. Losing weight, good for my figure, ha ha.

Suza. Thinking about her. Drifting. Altered state.

Perfect neutral state for

Open some windows.

Change sheets?

Tomorrow. Look for clean sheets. Big house?

Crazy idea for a pitch. Group of young adults with allergies, except their allergic reaction is to develop a superpower. Temporarily. Eat wheat, you're invisible. Handful of nuts, you can fly.

~~Green eggs, flames coming out of your~~

Rest time.

*Toothpaste. Add to foraging list. Don't want toothache now.

4th February

Better. Weak. Thrillers.

Crusoe?

Dine Out on the Garden is the book that I need to read.

When everything runs out, cans and all, I will need to know what I can pick and eat from what's growing naturally out there.

But don't go back to it just yet. Hide it.

~~Don't be in a hurry. Plan ahead, but it won't be for a while yet.~~

~~All the other recipe books. Useless already.~~

Maybe start small with just one thing from outside at a time.

Check everything against the pictures in the book. Only eat plants you're sure you can identify.

Enough food stored up for now. Start eating nature another day.

Sleep now.

Suza and I lived in a mews house in Kensington, cobbled mews, invasive jasmine around our front door and big windows to get the light in. Ground floor bedrooms, big open space upstairs. Not in Winter but in the middle of the year the sun would cut down through the skylight, in June vertical enough to touch the bottom of the stairs.

We kept the back windows open when we could, no balcony but a waist-high railing, fence, whatever, on which she had pots and trailing plants. We were overlooked by the houses opposite but we worked out the exact demarcation line on the carpet where we weren't overlooked any more. Behind it we could do what we liked ~~and I remember~~

One hot Summer, we dragged our mattress upstairs and slept for a week inside the open back windows, the cool air, the slanting sun in the mornings. A sparrow flew in, and from then on, for a while, Suza laid breadcrumbs on the railing. But birds thought they could fly in and then out at the other end. Hit the far window and then we had to coax them out.

Warm afternoons. So little movement in the air. The departing sunshine.

Sometimes, the television. Cushions against the front of the sofa. Takeaways. Who got to choose the film?

She told me she was pregnant.

Remembering.

Sleep now.

~~The *Titanic*. We talked about~~

5th February

I need to keep the fire lit and a stock of wood inside. Go back to the big house and get some different books. There were magazines. Attention span. *Toothpaste. Toothache. Sheets.*

Kettle over the fire? Hook?

Rest now. Another hour.

We did it all. Washed our hands, wore masks, washed our mouths out with mouthwash or (once) soapy water, kept our distance.

~~Look up that old story about a bird flying through a hall. Sparrow? Storm outside?~~

6th February

Who knew? Crusoe wrote a book called *A Journal of the Plague Year.* Defoe. Daniel Defoe. Surname when born was Foe and he was a "secret agent", says the intro. I like this guy.

Maybe sit outside in the sun for an hour.

"Dreadful deliverance," he calls it.

First thing on his island, he checked what he had, knife and a pipe, then he climbed a tree and spent a night in it.

Memo to self: you're doing better than he was.

Planning for illness. What needs to be within reach?

Knife and a pipe. We had plastic cards, cash money, and food in the freezer.

FOR THE RECORD. This from Crusoe:

"As to all the disputes, wranglings, strife, and contention, which has happen'd in the world ~~about religion~~, whether niceties in doctrine, or schemes of ~~church~~ government, they were all perfectly useless to us, as for ought I can yet see, they have been to all the rest in the world."

Delete religion and stick with government, and he could be talking about now.

Maybe call some big global summit and set targets for how we get through this. If there's anybody left.

~~Did people want this? To feel alive?~~

7th February

Failed this test. The food-poisoning challenge. But pass it next time.

Being ill. Being ready to be ill. Illness is a test. Think it through.

Medical supplies.

Weight loss!

Build up my strength.

8th February

Back to normal. But taking it slowly today. I need to think about this. Carefully.

What do I need within reach for when I'm ill? What about accidents?

~~I need to carry a knife.~~ I need to find a tool belt. ~~Or improvise one.~~

~~Laundry?~~ Clothes!

Rest.

~~How much time spent waiting for the government to tell us what to do and getting indignant with the government for telling us what to do?~~

~~While all along missing the truth that we needed to be looking out for ourselves.~~

~~Dependents. Suspension of belief in ourselves? Step further into Plato's cave. News report of light behind us, govt says lights ahead = idea?~~

9th February

The hospital?

NB: Books on first aid.

Too much death in the hospital still? Houses have medical supplies.

Pharmacies. Looted already? ~~Survivors if so may be hostile now. Hungry not pleased to see me.~~

I'm going to have to be careful.

Medical supplies.

<u>No</u> mushrooms.

Natural remedies. Read up on plants, et cetera. Penicillin from – mould? What? Making medicine a possibility?

What did people do before?

Anything in Crusoe? Read the rest of it!

Life expectancy.

~~If I fall and break my leg, I won't be able to~~
~~I need to think about how I would~~

Alone.

10th February

Chinese New Year

This is a bad situation.

Feeling lonely. Don't like it.

~~There must be people in isolated situations who haven't been infected. Maybe there are people who are immune. How find them? Let them find me? Safer!~~

Read Crusoe!

He was rescued.

Maybe a copy of *A Journal of the Plague Year* in the big house?

11th February

Nothing today. Better. Out of bed.

Generator. More fuel?

Thinking about the long term. When there's no more fuel.

I need to rig up some kind of water butt next to the vegetable beds.

Maybe just buckets.

Dreadful deliverance.

Is this depression?

This is NOT depression.

Survive. Or don't. Your choice.

Your gut's recovered.

Get your head together.

12th February

I want to write down footprints. Like a footprint in the sand. Tyre tracks. Or the hum of Chris and Ken coming by in their cart. Just about anything not natural.

But it was a voice.

"Anybody inside?"

A woman's voice.

"Anybody in Powder Cottage? Hello?"

"I'm here! Wait!"

I didn't realise straight away that I wasn't wearing what you'd call decent civilised. I came running out, breathless.

"I came to find out how you're getting on. Hope you don't mind."

This is a report.

She was standing there in a big green one-piece outfit with a clear facemask. Full-face clear.

Looking like I'd imagined rescue would look. Black gloves.

But just her, holding a pair of heavy-duty bolt-cutters in both hands, resting them on her shoulder.

No team of people come to bring back the world.

"Are you from the government?"

"No. I'm not." As though that was a reasonable question. "There's a consignment of these outfits. Round the back of–"

"Ah! Can you wait? Don't go! Don't go!"

"I can wait. I tore the sleeve getting under your tree, anyway."

I came back out wearing trousers and carrying two of the kitchen chairs.

She'd taken off the green outfit but not the facemask. I hadn't realised it was separate.

Jeans. Walking boots. Blue top. Hair back in a ponytail. The facemask.

A fresh open face that looked familiar although I didn't recognise her straight away. An expression that made me smile in return. *And feel safe.*

She'd been hot inside the green outfit.

Pushed it down and off over her boots. Left it scuffed and inside-out on the ground.

"I was part of your burial detail."

"My burial detail?"

"You seemed to know what you were doing."

She saw that I didn't recognise her.

"It's me. Melusie."

And when I still didn't…

"Melusie Evans. I was the agent for the cottage."

"This place?"

"I showed you around."

"Of course!"

And so on. We had a reunion.

Straight past estate agent tenant and go directly to "We're both alive!"

And we sort of know each other.

And then more cautiously to: what are we going to do about this?

14th February

The report version.

When Melusie Evans showed me the cottage, she was wearing a thick yellow scarf wrapped around her neck and up over her chin, and a knitted blue bobble hat crammed down under her hood. I could see just eyes, nose mouth. No facemask but social distance.

You were under layers and that duffel coat was bulky.

Not like when you came out of that green hazmat suit. Tall and in your own shape.

You were so wrapped up back then that I couldn't see you.

That's why I didn't recognise you.

15th February

We talked for a while, didn't we?

We sat outside on my two kitchen chairs and talked about what you'd seen and I'd seen. What we knew. Awkward at first, but starting to relax with each other.

~~For most of that first conversation I was anxious not to scare you. Seems ridiculous now, but that's how I felt.~~

What happened first was, the town went into lockdown overnight. No advance notice. You'd been working at home already by then, half-expecting it. Called the office on the first morning and didn't get a straight answer. "Managers were talking to managers, blah blah blah. I was already pretty well stocked up and I was okay for a few weeks' money, so I went for a run, stopped at the corner shop on the way home, and holed up. Did that for a while."

You were living in a ground-floor flat with a garden, not far from the centre of town. You had friends around the town, and you spoke to them about what a nuisance this was. You spent time in the garden and you went running.

"Did you stay in touch with people?"

"By phone, for a while. I knew from past experience that the job would come back to me."

It was just another lockdown. Except that it wasn't, and pretty soon, you realised it wasn't.

"We were in touch for some of it, but that stopped."

In the beginning, you watched the news and discussed the news; it was all about towns and cities locking down on their own. Then the lockdown went national. That didn't surprise you or your friends because you were already beginning to notice that it was different this time. The daily briefings started – and stopped.

"It was chaotic, but in the wrong way. Hospitals were overwhelmed – then they stopped talking about hospitals. They kept saying Stay In Your Homes, as if it was a slogan. Volunteers were going to – then the army, then the police were going to deliver groceries to the door. It was all panic-talk, as if they wanted us to believe they had a plan. No talk about essential workers."

Food stores emptied. Some remained open; some closed but left their doors open to avoid having their windows broken; some were looted. There was no resupply – once a shelf was empty, it stayed empty.

"We wished each other luck. Said we'd see each other on the other side."

People died in their homes. There was no help; the emergency number played a recorded message: stay in your homes. Ambulances and plain vans began to be attacked – they were collecting the dead. You saw police in riot gear from your window. There were fights in your street. Broken shop windows and looting.

You watched everything fall apart. On your screen, on your daily run, then walk, then brief excursion – until going out at all got to feel too dangerous – and outside your window. You closed your curtains and kept them closed.

"Then nobody picked up the phone," you said. "None of my friends were there anymore."

One day, there was smoke. Part of the town was on fire.

That night, for the first time in a week, your street was quiet.

"I couldn't stay where I was, so–"

You took your opportunity to move from your flat with the garden to a safer hiding-place.

"I went to another flat. I thought it would be

more secure."

"And was it?"

You stood up and walked away from me.

FOR THE RECORD. In that first conversation, I didn't push you. I didn't want to spook you. If you left something out, or didn't tell me – I didn't ask.

You were sharing painful memories.

And you were actually a person. Alive and sitting in front of me. You were so very much real. I'd reached a point – you'll know already if you read this far – at which I was beginning to wonder whether I was the only survivor. The only human being left.

You'd shared so much. And I didn't want to ~~break the spell~~ scare you away.

And then abruptly you didn't want to talk about the safer hiding place.

And despite all my being careful, I'd said the wrong thing. That was obvious.

I'm not stupid.

But I wasn't going to push you in that first conversation.

You stood up and walked away from me – across to where you could look down at the water.

"There used to be a riverboat," I told you. "With a commentary for the tourists."

"Did it annoy you?"

"I got used to it. Liked it, actually. And then one day it wasn't there anymore."

"And that was how you realised?"

"That was my first clue. Silence."

"Ah."

Again, it felt as though I'd said the wrong thing.

"I remember silence," you said eventually.

I waited.

"The noise and the panic went on, and then there was silence. Suddenly, overnight. Like snow falling – waking up, you know, and there's snow on the ground?"

And then you were talking again. The smoke had cleared days before, you told me – the fire must have burned itself out – but the air by then had gone very bad.

You told me about wrapping up. As much against the smell as against the plague.

About hearing the backhoe.

About seeing – that must have been me – on the street. Then others as well.

Seeing us bringing out the bodies.

All of us wrapped up and working together – but keeping a distance from each other.

You watched us.

When you were ready, you joined us.

You told me that whole story, standing there on the other side of the path, gradually looking more at me than the river, and then abruptly you clammed up again.

I could see it in your face.

The thing you didn't want to remember.

I'm not stupid. I made a guess (that turned out to be wrong).

~~I wanted to know.~~

~~But more than that,~~ I was pretty sure that talking about it would help you to get past it.

I wanted to hear it because if you said it out loud I could try to help you with it.

But not that day.

So I broke the silence by finishing up the story of the riverboat – how regular it was, how I'd

thought of taking the trip, gone down to see it pass
– seeing it, waving to the people on it; I made all
that up – and about how it messed up my routine
to realise that I hadn't heard it.

I talked about living in the cottage, and blah
blah blah, and you made an effort to look as though
you were listening.

You were amazed that I'd been so isolated from
it all, you told me.

But you know the cottage, I said. Why wouldn't
I be isolated?

You kind of laughed.

I'd had absolutely no idea that any of it was
happening, I said.

You came back and sat down.

You said something about how peaceful it was.

I offered you a mug of tea.

Then you suddenly jolted up and said you had
to go.

I watched you leave.

Then I picked up the green outfit, duct-taped
the tear, and hung it up inside.

Emptied the pockets.

16th February

You were wary. Cautious. Obviously.

Traumatised by whatever it was.

You didn't tell me about the tent.

But you left me while it was still light and ~~I said
nothing because~~ and then you came back the next
morning.

You'd said you would. I was still relieved. I
wasn't sure you would. *I wanted you to come back.

I didn't guess about the tent exactly. I thought

69

you might have stayed overnight at the big house.

Believe me, I did think of asking you to stay here, but I could see that something bad had happened and I didn't want to spook you. ~~See above.~~

~~I didn't want you to think I was~~

I could see that you were holding yourself together.

And it seemed to me that coming out of hiding to talk to me like that, just walking up to the cottage and calling out, must have taken some doing. I was respectful of that ~~although I've worked out since that I should have been scared of you.~~ *Sorry. Just meant, what you were carrying, the bolt-cutters, knife, pepper spray, et cetera. ~~Not referring to~~*

So I suppose what I'm saying is, I didn't want to come out with anything ~~because you might take it as~~ for fear of coming out with the wrong thing.

And especially, I didn't want to come on all Old Guys Are Protective with somebody who ~~had learned~~ already knew a lot more about survival than I did.

I don't think I've explained this very well. I just wanted you to see that first meeting from my ~~POV~~ point of view.

17th February

I think you were sounding me out, weren't you? To come in on your own terms. *I get that. Okay.*

Then, in the morning, you came back and I made coffee. We sat out in the sun again. The atmosphere was different. You were less wary and I was too.

I don't know how to put this, but you were ready for the question. I could kind of feel it.

"I'm sorry I left so abruptly," you said. "It's just–"

"Bad memories."

"It was awful."

And then we both just kind of waited.

You might have started speaking, and I would have listened, but it felt right to say, "Where did you live, after you left your flat with the garden?"

You didn't say anything for a moment. Looking at the trees across the path. Then you looked at me and looked away again.

I thought I'd said the wrong thing again, but–

"Empty rental flat. People could never find the entrance when they were viewing."

You looked down as you said that. Used your finger to draw an invisible box on the knee of your jeans.

"Safe place?"

"I thought it was."

Ah.

We didn't say anything after that. *You weren't wrong. The burial detail didn't find your front door.*

Eventually–

"Did you come here looking for me? Or for a place to stay?"

~~That came out wrong. I felt it at the time.~~

"Because you'd be welcome, I mean."

"I don't want you to think."

I said, "You'd be safe here."

She said, "I thought of you out here. I thought there was a chance."

And we sat there, young, thin, beautiful woman and old guy who'd come out first with a towel between his legs and held up front and back by a tool-belt round his waist. ~~*My trousers were wearing out. I was improvising. You know this.~~

And we just sat there, the rest of the conversation you we needed to have somehow no longer urgent – you'd told me enough; the rest could wait.

And then you stood up and you bent forward and you kissed me on the forehead.

In that moment I felt like I could be your father.

~~So that was cl~~

Melusie Evans.

I nearly wrote "young thin beautiful woman who had hoped to find the cottage empty" but let's put that behind us now, shall we? You felt guilty enough to confess it, but it's never been a thing for me. Obvious thought to have, in the circumstances.

18th February

We used to talk about the "male gaze", remember?

No, that was Suza.

Back in this book again. Time passes and the date on the page says I'm a day later.

So many days hidden between pages.

Suza and I used to talk about the "male gaze". Suza did.

You and I, we don't talk about the male gaze. We have time to laugh, that's what matters.

I write this on a warm Autumn day. You're outside breaking up kindling and I'm sitting at the table where we finished the jigsaw, watching you through the glass.

The male gaze. Do you remember when you turned up in that green outfit and I was wearing a towel and a belt?

You're in a sleeveless Summer dress now, it's a Liberty print, and trainers.

I'm in cargo pants, you called them, work trousers with knee-pads and pockets, with my tool belt slung around my hips, and the big builder-braces with the elephants on to hold up the trousers.

My "lumberjack shirt" if I need a jacket. Steel toecaps on my boots, although if I'm honest, now that I've got them I need to wear them in more. Not comfortable yet.

We can laugh at ourselves. Fancy dress from the big house and maintenance. From that one run we made into town.

You had never heard of the Village People. Funny, though.

~~Male gaze. Although that was all about strangers. Not~~

~~I'm here to write. You're busy. I'm busy.~~

~~The ends of these days are so beautiful. With the "bistro table" and both of us exercised, really healthily tired~~

19th February

We talked about living in the big house in the Winter. Bad weather. Decided not.

FOR THE RECORD: Melusie tells me that after I stopped turning up, the funerals stopped happening. Me starting up the backhoe had been the start of it? I think? We gathered somehow, must have been that, and then there were several days on which we didn't – I didn't come every day, so no surprise, but

Too much detail.

Several days I didn't come and then one day she came out to see if she could see anybody, and that was her mistake.

She was holed up safely with a routine of late-night forages to the broken-open stores to stock up only when necessary. Beginning to think about the future, escaping from town altogether, but holed up safe enough.

Nobody had realised she was female.

She says now, working it out.

She'd relaxed a bit, with the air clearer, and

Her story. Not mine to tell. *I will tear this page out if you want me to.*

She had moved to an upstairs studio flat with narrow stairs down to a ground-level front door. She'd tipped a chest of drawers down the stairs to block the front door. When she wanted to get out, she had to climb over the chest of drawers and push it back up the first few stairs to open the door. Wedge it in place so she could get back in again.

"It would have been so much simpler if I'd just put a broom handle, or something, between the door and the opposite wall."

She tells me now.

As a way of getting herself to talk about the painful memory. Working up to it.

She almost laughs at herself, telling me about the wardrobe and the trouble getting out of her own front door.

Then the laughter goes away.

Outside the front door was a narrow alleyway. A very narrow alleyway, coming out between two shops on Minchin Street. If you noticed it at all, you'd think it was just the gap between the two buildings.

"Real hide-out territory. It didn't go anywhere. No reason for anybody to walk down it."

She'd been seen. And followed.

Not mine to tell.

But Melusie, if you hadn't ~~ki~~ hurt him, he would have hurt you.

20th February

Panic. Shock. Understandable reactions.

She'd actually had a car ready. Her shared car from the agency, with the logo on the side, parked near the agency but she had the key.

She had loaded it up over several nights, early on in the lockdown, with the tent and basics.

~~Planning ahead. Being prepared.~~

With the idea of a holiday.

"I thought, if I got really stir-crazy with staying at home in the lockdown, I could drive off to a field I know, near a beach, and spend some time there. Nobody would know."

Miracle nobody trashed the car, in the bad time.

~~White panels for the logo instead of back windows. Cheap car. Nobody could see in. Too much info.~~

After the attack, she panicked. No thought of camping now. She went straight to the car and drove out North, heading inland. Circled round.

She'd had me in the back of her mind all along.

Correction – keep it real – she'd had Powder Cottage in mind all along.

Thinking through their property list. Second homes, rentals, remote properties likely to be empty. Properties for the long term.

She knew I was there but hadn't expected me to be alive. ~~That was a conversation. We really broke the ice with that one.~~

She parked at the gate. She had the green outfit in the car but she took a spade from maintenance. For me. She thought of burying me. I was touched when she told me that. ~~We should pick a plot for~~

When she realised that I was alive – saw smoke, watched, saw me – she camped. Set up her tent and watched me.

For days.

Until she was ~~as~~ sure ~~as she could be~~.

She was armed when she came up to the Cottage and called out. Heavily weaponised. Lots of pockets in that green outfit. The bolt-cutters were heavy on her shoulder but she could swing them up in her two hands and let them fall.

I should have felt vulnerable when she first appeared outside the cottage. Should have been scared.

~~She hadn't taken long to realise that I was harmless.~~

~~She'd had an impression of me already from showing me the cottage, and she'd been watching me for several days.~~

~~I don't think it had occurred to her to~~

She'd known for certain that I wasn't a threat to her – she tells me now – within a second of my coming out of the cottage.

I'd come "capering out" – she tries to tell me about it, but she just laughs. Really laughs. Goes into it, cupping her mouth and nose.

Shirt. Belt and towel. Apparently, I was also wearing slippers and a hat made of a folded sheet of torn-off wallpaper from the big house.

I like that hat. But I don't think I was wearing it back then.

But okay.

Worn-out underwear. Sunburn. Cold stone underfoot.

Yeah, I can laugh at myself.

Melusie, you've just looked up, seen me in the window, and waved.

We're going swimming.

When you read this – this is the point at which I came out and told you to stop working because we're going swimming.

FOR THE RECORD. It never occurred to me to wonder if I could trust you. Maybe I should have been more cautious. Maybe I'm complacent by nature, maybe a man doesn't think that way, but I say my instincts were good from the start. I've always trusted you, Melusie.

21st February

That was good. A happy time. ~~You're so beautiful.~~

Warm, clear water and sunbathing after, drying off together on the deserted beach.

No, I didn't need my towel, thank you for mentioning it.

FOR THE RECORD. That yacht, sideways on the rocks. Flat-calm tide not moving it.

Crusoe would have plundered it.

Deserted beach, deserted world.

We haven't seen anybody, in any direction.

When Melusie left town, there were very few

survivors left. [Ref. my theory: we're the loners, not immune.]

If there are survivors, scavengers, they haven't come this way, but we keep our eyes open and we've blocked the road from the big house, chainsaw as well this time but made it look like a natural fall, laid some booby traps and alarms. They can't get near the cottage without us knowing.

22nd February

We went into town one last time. We took my car, bigger, parked past the roadblock now, and as usual we circled round to come in from another direction. Needn't have bothered.

The air in town is clear now.

The air's clear, the sky's clear, the sky was blue with wispy white clouds. I parked in the sports-centre car park and you were amused that I parked neatly in a slot, between the white lines. There were other cars, but all of them dead. We stood for a moment at the machine – I remember that moment, like it was something to stop for, a memorial even; we looked at each other; "Card payments only," you said and it was funny-absurd-tragic – then we walked down the long steps. The pay machine. Stations of the walk into town. Instinctive stop.

The backhoe's where I left it. The big graves have settled a bit but on the positive side grass is growing and there are some flowers.

Clear, fresh air. Worth inhaling. The air's even fresher here, but there was something about breathing fresh air in town. Like it was over. Rainbow.

We sat for a while on a bench by the river, faces up to the sky, breathing in the air.

That was like an old-time moment, like we might have walked down to the river in a lunchbreak and eaten a bought sandwich on the bench.

We walked along the path. Saw nobody on either side.

Heard nothing but the water. *I don't remember any ducks?*

Mass of supermarket trolleys in the weir. A scum of rubbish.

"You want to do this?"

"I think we have to."

"We could go somewhere else?"

You looked at me. "Let's just do it."

I get it now. You wanted to get past what happened.

Overlay the memory with another visit.

~~And we needed stuff. Forget the psychodrama. We needed stuff.~~

We went back to the car and drove over the bridge into town.

The silence was the first thing when we stopped this time. You had told me about it. Down here, not even a breeze ~~although maybe that's memory playing a trick~~. I remembered you telling me about the silence, and yes, I was prepared for it but I was struck by it even so. Not a big echoing silence or a dramatic silence, not a special effect or even just a no-riverboat silence, and there were birds, but when we turned the car off and opened the doors, we were sitting in an emptiness where all our senses said there should be noise or bustle or at least something – just some kind of background people-disturbance that wasn't there.

I remember the feeling that went with it. That it grew into. We've talked about this too. "~~The Void.~~" As if we were reaching out with our senses and the ~~next step~~ connection wasn't there.

You felt it the same way, although you were prepared for it. The place in our heads where we just take it for granted that we're not alone. We tick off the little cues – but this time they weren't there.

It was like a feeling of being in a place that wasn't there. Figure on a screen, no background. Difficult to put into words. As if the town had stopped being a town.

The street signs still had words on them and those words were legible.

But everything else – couldn't read it. ~~Read any meaning into it? Get any sense out of it?~~

Maybe it was in our heads. No such thing as a town anymore.

Stillness like the heartbeat gone out of a body.

~~It was shocking. A little grief mixed in.~~

~~Too much. Delete some of this.~~

You said, "Look at the cars."

The dead cars.

~~The end of civilisation.~~

~~No! Keep it real. Shorten this and tone it down. Just – for the record.~~ *This is real.

Windscreens filmed over with dirt, paintwork the same greyed-out shade as the roads, the houses. Took me a moment to notice, but – all the flat tyres.

And then you said that thing about the rubbish.

There wasn't much, or maybe it was just scattered evenly.

The birds had continued the looting.

You said, "This is the kind of rubbish that rubbish leaves behind."

Scattered, dried out, decayed, faded to dirt-grey.

Broken windows, doors open.

Nature coming back. Those cats.

We must have cleared so many bodies ~~back when we were doing that.~~

None left.

~~Maybe one.~~

~~He can stay where he is.~~

23rd February

That was how the town felt. It slowed us down and we've discussed it since. I'm writing it down but I can't quite put my finger on how it was.

Cathartic. For us, do I mean? Not really. Final confirmation of the apocalypse. The end, stamped and dated. Something like that.

More like: the thing had happened. We were characters still on stage after the play had ended. We were still characters but the props were just cardboard now.

Sluggish with the feel of it, the shock, the pressure, but busy and nervy and in a hurry to get out. That's how we were. We were slowed-down and spooked, all at once.

We parked on a double-yellow line on Oddley Street, just short of a bus stop.

Right outside Harkins. The big doors were hooked open and we could see display counters, racks, broken mirrors. Natural light only, and not much of it.

"Even if the lifts are working…"

"No lifts."

We both carried hammers and I had the shotgun.

We locked the car.

Up to home furnishings. Household. Bed stuff. Pillows, duvets in boxes. Sheets.

~~Some of this we could have found at the big house but you wanted it new.~~

No people, no bodies.

Toiletries. Pharmacy. Toothpaste. Woman stuff.

~~Melusie, I love that the bedroom, bathroom have your things, two of us, part of not being alone is all your unfamiliar clutter.~~

Filled a pillowcase with things from off the shelves, the floor, and behind the counter in the pharmacy. We have new underwear now. Washing line. *Moisturiser! *Sun-tan lotion!

Crunching glass underfoot. No interruption. The store not a familiar place anymore; it was full of its own emptiness, and dark.

A man/woman watched us leaving from the end of the street. Wrapped.

First living person. Only one.

We both saw him as we came out of Harkins for the last time. He ducked back but then he realised that we'd seen him and stepped out.

We stood looking at each other. No move to come closer, no move to wave.

You made a sound like flicking him away and went to the car.

He stepped back out of sight,

We drove out of town the wrong way, heading inland. ~~Somebody watching us so precaution worthwhile after all.~~

FOR THE RECORD. You suggested we take the opportunity to look around. ~~Couldn't see him when we passed his corner. You didn't even look.~~

So we did that, although not for long. We wanted to get ourselves gone.

Clear streets only. Saw no people. Rats.

"As the world collapses, people put their bins out," you said, after we passed one street of terraced houses.

~~We drove out of town, through villages, briefly the motorway.~~

~~The roadblock on the motorway. Deserted.~~

~~It's as if~~ there's nobody left. There really is nobody left.

Just that one man/woman in town.

"We've got a good thing here," you said on the way home.

"Don't talk to strangers?" I said.

"Let's not throw this away."

Agreed.

We are in hiding and that's how we behave.

No strangers.

Left the car behind a hedge outside the roadblock.

We carried everything overland to the cottage.

Saw the tent. You showed it to me. I suggested that we stay there some night.

24th February

Last entry a month ago.

We moved the tent. Treeline above the beach, view of the docks on the other side.

Planned a night watching for lights. Or movement. Or something.

In the evening we walked down to T.H.'s bench. I told you about T.H. and you thought it was funny.

Then you said it was sweet and you kissed me.

"What's that for?"

"I don't know, I just."

A different kiss. Slower. Then you stood up.

"Melusie. Wait."

"What?"

Laughter in your voice. Teasing.

"I want to—"

"Here? Really?"

Never really darkness at night. Never really cold.

We meant to watch for lights.

But we just lay out under the stars after, talking and (mostly) not talking, until it was time to curl in together and sleep.

I call it after. You say it's part of it.

25th February

Visit to the big house. Chair, sofa. I keep my leather chair. We have outdoor furniture now.

More vegetable beds. More planting. We are farmers now.

Nobody to see.

FOR THE RECORD. Decision. We stay here in the cottage until/unless there's a reason to do otherwise. We go out if we have to, foraging or whatever, but we don't look for people, and if we see any, we stay out of sight. Change our mind later, discuss it, but first reaction: hide.

The cottage is solid, secure, warm, and if we're

careful, the fire makes hardly any smoke. We forage for wood now, and stack it around the fireplace and inside. We're almost through the big house's and maintenance's supply of logs. In the house and round the sheds.

We're safest if we're never found. But there are boards for the windows now and the front door is solid. We keep the weapons in the house.

We shouldn't think this way, but now that we've thought this way, I think we can begin to relax.

26th February

Woke up to snow. Dull light. Lifted the tent flap, and snow. Perhaps an inch.

We've been coming up here these past few weeks, to spy on the docks. Watch the streetlights fail, one by one, the stubborn automated systems.

We've talked about the yachts in the marina, idea of sailing off somewhere, or just camping on one for a while. We've watched them, picking which we'd have.

A couple more have slipped their moorings and been wrecked, one has sunk on its mooring. Couple just gone.

The day we went fishing and found that plastic rowboat.

Write that for the record!

Decided fishing from the pontoon was safer.

Although the wood's rotting.

That day we woke up to snow.

We lay in the tent, flap back, warm in our big duvets, and watched the snow.

Is this global warming? Do we get a snow season now?

Or just a global cleaning away? Whitewashing everything that went before.

We packed up, tent and all, and headed back to the cottage.

~~Brought in more logs. My system: dry logs go onto the fire; damp logs to replace the dry logs around the fire; wet logs brought in from outside and put in the place of the damp logs. That way we maintain a constant supply of dry logs for the fire.~~
I KNOW you laugh at me. But it works.

FOR THE RECORD. We were down at the pontoon, watching a shoal of mackerel ~~fizzing~~ ~~boiling~~ bubbling up the water. ~~Disturbing the surface.~~ We were fishing, throwing out feathers on the end of a line. Caught six. We've set up a barbecue outside now, down by the water. You gut them, I cook them, we take turns. There are more fish than there used to be, I'm sure of it. Fishing can't be this ~~easy~~ reliable.

(We spend warm evenings down there now, on the edge of the water, wafting charcoal-smoke downriver, barbecuing whatever we catch, and mostly there's something, and you're keen to boil up seaweed as a vegetable. So far, so okay – tastes good; no challenge. We're a couple of nut-brown people, dressed in whatever. I wonder what the old riverboat would say, as it passed us.)

You pointed out the rowing boat on the other side, tied up under the spread of a tree over the water. Still afloat, although pressed down into the water with every high tide. Miracle it wasn't sunk, I said.

We swam over.

Plastic boat. Full of water when we got close to

it. But double-skinned. Never going to sink. Oars pushed into the branches above the water level. Rowlocks in place.

We swam over on an evening when we thought it was low tide. That gave us a shorter swim although we had to squidge through more mud on the far side ~~(swam from the pontoon our side = whoever is going to read this, that I have to be so precise?)~~. Pulled the boat from under the tree, tipped it to get the water out.

"Ugh!" Green seaweed and slime and wriggling water-things. On the underside, more green stuff, plus blobby moving wriggly things with half-formed fish (?) inside. Weed like cress on a flannel, drenched. More green than that – like bright spinach? ~~I remember finding shark's eggs as a boy.~~

We were naked from the swimming and we'd brought nothing with us, so used leaves and dried seaweed from the shoreline, clumps of stuff, to wipe it down enough and wipe ourselves down, each other, we were so muddy, we were laughing, splashing, slept after – and when we were finished with all that we were ready to go back, so we got in the boat and pushed off with the idea that Plan A – we'd float out to the middle and give ourselves a rowing lesson – could wait for another day.

Plan B was – we were ready to go straight across, tie the boat up to the pontoon, ~~take a bath~~ splash-around in the river, and get back to the cottage.

We've laughed about it since, but my guess is, we were lucky.

We must have swum across just as the tide was turning. Or just after. Slack tide?

By the time we were ready to row go back across in the boat, the tide was going out. It was flowing quite fast, and it caught the boat.

We went off downriver at something faster than walking pace, the trees gliding past, and however effectively we rowed (you'd done it before, ~~thank~~) we couldn't get out of the current.

Eventually, just as we were coming round the kink in the river before it opens out, you managed to grab a branch and pull us in.

We walked back.

We could have been swept out to sea.

We fish from the pontoon.

27th February

This cottage is so beautiful now. The bunches of lavender hanging from the laundry thing in the kitchen. Other herbs(?). The light seems clearer. *I'm not stupid. You cleaned the ~~skylight~~ kitchen roof. How? WHEN?*

I hadn't realised the mess until you cleared it. Thank you for not being indignant. Yes, I am doing my share. Will continue to do it. *I'm thinking of the past again. Don't suppose I'll ever stop.*

Have we been to the big house for the last time? FOR THE RECORD we did talk about living there. ~~Again?~~ Still empty, still standing, you went round and closed the windows to a crack.

Too conspicuous, you said. Too vulnerable.

There can't be much else that we need to bring across. *Yes, it does make me happy that we've got a medicine cabinet. But okay – I'll stop talking about it.*

You were right that we needed to bury them. Among the roses in the walled garden.

At peace. ~~I know what that means now.~~

28th February

Gave myself a scare.

FOR THE RECORD. Walked out late, last thing. Heard something and turned on the flashlight and there were eyes looking at me.

So many eyes, reflecting the light.

A herd of deer. Small deer. Muntjaks(sp?), Melusie says. *Dictionary. Reference books. More shelves. Shed? Big house/maintenance.*

She came out and they didn't run away. Flashlight off, light of the moon, they gathered round stood watching us, not scared off.

Struck me I was the one who'd been scared. Of people might be out there? Ghosts?

Nature is safe from us now.

29th February

How much of this was self-preservation and how much was loneliness and how soon was it love?

Remember when we rigged up the cans and the fishing lines? The tripwires and alarms around our own stockade?

I remember the day you told me you felt safe.

~~That was the day you~~

We started off with me in the bed (you saying no you're okay on the floor) and you in the yoga mat/sleeping bag combo you brought with you. Remember?

You were in the bedroom from the start. You really didn't like being alone ~~but I remember you curled up in the far~~

You're kind and lovely. And warm. I'm not very

~~demanding needful~~ lively. I'm sorry that I'm not younger.

Enough said about that. We're friends and companions and a team and we get along.

There are two chairs in the cave now.

If I tear these last pages out, you'll wonder. This is me being honest. Weak and strong. What you want and not. My love.

*Melusie, if you read this, if you get this far, I've been honest. Just honest. I want you to know me. I'm glad you're with me, and thank you for everything, and let's fill the rest of these pages together. I do love you. Yes.

I know you've been sick these past few mornings. Tell me when you're ready to talk because I want to ~~help share~~ help you through ~~be part of the future we're making together~~ this. Be a father again. I'm here with you.

Did you pick up a test, that last day we went into town?

We'll go to that beach soon, and I'll show you the rock and the waves.

I see the three of us playing there one day.

St. David's Day (Wales)

1st March

~~This is his~~

2nd March

~~I remember his~~

3rd March

He was a lovely man. He was very kind and very clever.

He helped me when our Mishka was born and despite a lot of panic and nonsense the birth was successful. Mishka is so healthy and beautiful. We couldn't weigh him but he was so obviously strong. He has blue eyes and his hair is lightened by being out in the sun so much.

He wanted to take me off to find a hospital and doctors but I told him no. I told him I trusted him. There are no doctors. He knew that but he was anxious.

He was quite helpful and I think we were lucky. If there is a God, after all this, she was on our side. He read his books and more books he found in the old house, but I told him women had been doing this since before books.

Mishka and I will stay here until he is grown, and when I have finished teaching him all I can he might go searching for the rest of the world. We have seen nobody but perhaps he will find a partner or there is a partner out there.

Let him not be lonely.

4th March

His serious notebooks I have put safely away. Perhaps there will be people to find them one day.

This book is for Mishka to read. I shall read it to Mishka and teach him to read.

The parts about me are quite accurate although I didn't realise he saw me that way.

He told me he started this book before he knew

what was happening. He wanted it to be a first attempt at his book about his wife Suzanne and his son Eddie. I feel I know Suzanne a little from how he was with me and he knew how to be a father.

He was my partner in life and I loved him.

5th March

I have carved his initials on the bench next to T.H.'s brass plate. I sit there sometimes with Mishka. We used to sit there together while I fed Mishka.

I buried him at the top, in the open, with the sunshine and the view of the sea. All the stars he liked to watch. All the light that looked like darkness, he used to say to me. Mishka and I sleep up there in the tent when the nights are warm. I feel that he knows that we are there, and that we know that he is with us.

6th March

We went to that beach, to find the rock and the waves.

We saw nobody. Not on the roads, not on the beach.

That was the last of our fuel.

7th March

We sat against that rock and he told me about his past. I told him about mine.

There was no rain.

He took Mishka to the edge of the sea and they splashed together in the surf. Mishka was delighted. They were both laughing and I was laughing too when I joined them.

That is how I remember him. Beside me, holding our baby, with the sun in the sky and the sea shining with light.

The making of
Escape Mutation

A Journal of the Plague Years

Special Feature

This is a short book, some 20,000 words, so I thought I'd provide some extras – such as you'd find if you bought a film on DVD, for example.

Escape Mutation *happens close to where I live, so I write about the locations (and how I've adjusted the geography) and the settings (which were also fun to dream up). I'm still curious about the people in the story, so I've imagined actors to discuss the characters they played. You might also want a few hints as to what happens next?*

Note: spoilers ahead. Read Escape Mutation *before you read any further. These extras are just ever so slightly tongue-in-cheek, but if you've enjoyed this book so far, I hope you find the additional information interesting.* **WE**

Contents

On location

"Take the circular walk round Argal Lake near Penryn in Cornwall. Start from the car park and go counter-clockwise around the lake. Pretty soon, you'll come to a cottage-sized recess carved in the stone to your right. That's the location we chose for Powder Cottage.

It's wet though, in that recess, and the brief included a dry environment, a footpath wide enough for a golf cart, and a slope down to a river.

So we dried out the recess and transposed it to an unreliable memory of the walk at Trelissick Gardens near Truro. We put it on the path just at the point where you can look down through the trees and see the mussel farm on the Truro River – close to the King Harry Ferry.

We had to remove the mussel farm and the ferry, of course, to make space for the riverboat when it was running (in the pre-production phase of the book), but there is a pontoon and we kept that.

The walk around the headland approximates roughly to the walk at Trelissick Gardens, but the setting for T.H.'s bench has been re-imagined from the walk around the playing fields at Boscawen Park near Truro (those playing fields are also the site of the mass graves, although for that purpose they've been moved to Lemon Quay and the Truro River has been re-routed down Lemon Street).

When they sit on T.H.'s bench, or camp

overnight on the headland, the characters are looking across the water at Falmouth, with additional moored yachts brought across from Mylor. The direct view from T.H.'s bench to Falmouth required a significant redrawing of the map and accounted for much of the location budget. For a real-life approximation to that view of Falmouth, go to the headland above Flushing Beach. You'll have to bring your own bench.

"Maintenance" was based on the works area at Boscawen Park, and the exteriors of the Big House were an amalgam of several National Trust and privately owned properties in the South West. The rose garden from the short story *Beautiful Roses*, which shows up in the collection *God – The Interview and other stories*, and which is itself a self-contained extract from the novel *The Journey from Heaven*, by the same author, was repurposed as the burial place for the deceased family found in the Big House. They rest peacefully.

The town combined elements of Truro, Edinburgh and Bath. On the characters' last trip into town, they parked just past the bus stop on St David Street, Edinburgh, going up from Prince's Street. If you're looking for Harkins, you'll find it on Prince's Street – but that was a relatively small adjustment to the geography. There were some challenging issues around scale, given that wide Edinburgh Streets don't fit easily into narrow West Country towns.

The remembered childhood beach is Rockham

Beach, near Mortehoe in Devon. We moved it down the coast to an accessible location just South of Holywell Bay, Cornwall. Easier to reach, after he's gone, for a mother and baby."

Set design

"We wanted an almost womb-like feel to Powder Cottage, although at the outset we also wanted it to be very obviously a place where a man lived alone. Some of that clutter is deliberate!

We made the decision early on to throw realism out of the window – this was going to be a holiday cottage like no other. The colour palette is mostly browns and muted shades of ochre, and I'm sure you'll have noticed how many of the props – see that lamp? – are junk-shop antiques.

We used a lot of old wood – beams, floorboards, all this mismatched furniture. The dining table came from a junk shop and his leather armchair we actually found on a skip.

Uh, yeah, we might have let him believe that it came from a charity shop. But – no.

The open fire was a gift – we could stack logs to add to the overall effect. The exposed stone surfaces are notionally white, but we used an ochre/cream blend of paint to keep the room dark.

It is a holiday cottage, though, we couldn't get totally away from that, so for example he had to have a wide-screen TV and an Xbox. All the modern gadgets. But we kept those out of his line of sight so that they don't intrude into the story. He brings his own laptop and Moleskine notebooks and doesn't watch TV, did you notice that? Not once! Never mind realism; I count that as a success.

By the way, you'll notice that the paperback

books and the jigsaw are shelved rather more prominently than you'd expect in a real holiday cottage. What can I tell you? It worked.

William was very specific about the titles he wanted on the bookshelves, and that took up some time. One of the special-effects guys actually had to sit down and write *Dine Out on the Garden*, which of course doesn't exist in the real world. We were surprised at how many newsreaders offered to write thrillers for us.

Upstairs – we went for the same theme, but lighter. The thinking was, we wanted an area of the house where they could come together without either of them having to compromise their individuality. Melusie's arrival brings light, we decided, as a simple, perhaps even subliminal, marker of the difference between them. She also very much represents outdoors – well, they both do, but differently.

She's seen through his eyes for most of the book, so, you know, the idea was, she brings a lightness to his mind. He's not alone any more. When she arrives - did you notice how the tree cover thins out when the attention is on her? She gets more sunlight? That was tricky to achieve, but it was worth it. Does something to the mood, right?

We lightened the paint between the beams upstairs, and you'll notice – I think we got away with this – that the windows are slightly larger. There's altogether a less cluttered feel up here – and yes, you guessed it, those open shelves are designed to fill up with duvets, sheets, bright things, after their last trip into town. They're a team by then, and, yeah, partners.

He doesn't write about that side of their relationship, because actually he wouldn't, but I think William's set it up so that you can read between the lines. At first it's awkward, obviously, but by the end – well. They come to love each other. They have a child. Over to you.

Powder Cottage was the primary set, where we spent most of our time and budget, but we also had to put together sets for the interiors of the Big House, when he breaks in, and for the mews house in London – for the flashbacks. The mews house was easy – a very minimalist space, big windows, jasmine, framed posters, cobbled street outside – but the Big House – well, I think it works.

Most of it – well, we just used what was there. William has a memory – get him to show it to you – of visiting a museum with a glass roof over the hallway and staircase, and the upstairs corridors and rooms are what he remembers of a house where friends of his once lived. The big modern kitchen – actually, I'm not sure I should tell you this. It's the kitchen of a house in Islington. Yes, London.

And I know it's supposed to be modern, but we had to go back all the way to 1984 to get it. There's a mural of a vine up one wall and across the ceiling, but he doesn't even mention that.

Tricks of the trade, eh? I really enjoyed working

on *Escape Mutation*. I think we all did. And *Dine Out on the Garden* is doing really well, which is weird, right? I'll see if I can get Alex to autograph a copy for you."

The Cast

"This was a gift of a role. I was on the page from the start all the way through almost to the finish, and the narration, unreliable or not, was all mine. I had the character to myself, his back story, his motivation, his whole story arc.

What I found so fascinating was the challenge of playing a character with no name. Literally a blank canvas. I discussed this with William, and he agreed with my suggestion that I could give the character a name, privately, without disclosing it, and I did that.

Would you believe, it made a difference? I'm not sure how, but it did. So I think I can say that I'm the only person who knows the true name of the leading character in *Escape Mutation*! Not even the author knows it, isn't that interesting?

Oh no, absolutely not – the whole idea was that the character should remain nameless, although I believe there is one reference? To a family name? I don't remember. But I'm afraid I couldn't possibly – sorry. Perhaps I should reveal it on my deathbed.

I created the character, yes, I think you can say that. William and I spoke at length in the pre-write about who we thought he was, what his burdens and motivations were, how he would – yes, even how he would face the task of writing his own life story, but after that, I immersed myself in the role. It was mine and I will always be grateful for that."

"When William first sent me the manuscript for *Escape Mutation*, I knew immediately that I wanted the role. It wasn't just that the book was unfinished back then, so that there was so much still open to explore. It was Melusie herself. She has such potential as a character.

Let me see. Melusie Evans. Her back story is that she's a small-town estate agent. She's intelligent and practical, that's her background. But was she content? Was she ambitious? Given the potential that she finds in herself – she's a fighter; she's a survivor – how does she feel about finding her true self? Without the plague, she would never have known who she could be.

She's self-reliant, yes, and exactly, she's capable of protecting herself aggressively when necessary. But at heart, I think, she's open to companionship. The one wish she expresses for her son is that he not be lonely. She finishes the book as a mother, after all, after we've watched a loving relationship develop.

She's entirely depicted by a man, yes, and of course man-writes-woman can be problematic. I don't think it was so much a problem in this case, although William and I did discuss it – you can ask him about that – because in a way that's the whole point: the whole book's dictated by an isolated man. You could argue that Melusie's not directly depicted at all. You're explicitly looking at his impressions. Until the end, of course.

You could say it's all him – but I'd say it isn't. I

found it interesting to work with a strong, complex, vulnerable, dominant character who is nevertheless only seen through the eyes of a man. She's such a strong character – strong in every sense – and what I found most satisfying was the challenge of finding the real woman in the portrayal.

I think there's a strength in it, actually. Yes, really. I get to perform the role, and my character gets to manipulate, although I'm not sure that's the right word, the narrator. Unreliable narrator; he's pretty stir-crazy by the time she turns up. And we leave it to the reader to work out who she is, who he is, and trace the relationship as it develops between the lines."

Writing *Escape Mutation*:
An interview with William Essex

"This was my lockdown project, did I tell you?
We were all freshly locked down and talking about
how we were going to read the classics, write the
novels, re-organise our lives, use the time – and
then the inertia set in.

Must have been some time around mid-
April 2020, maybe, coming over us like a fog.
Lockdown was boring after all, we weren't getting
anything done, the virus wasn't going away and
those nightly government briefings were getting
just a bit repetitive. I started writing.

It wasn't going anywhere at first. I didn't plan
it, I didn't tidy it up, but pretty soon I began to get
a feel for the guy telling the story – the narrator, I
should call him. He's not me, although I've given
him a couple of my memories. He became real as
I amped up his isolation and then he took on a
personality all of his own.

It's a book about him, really. The disaster
happens almost entirely offstage. It slowly dawns
on him that something's wrong just as the virus
crept up on us. Yes, and if you're reading it for
the disaster, it's a slow start – like the virus;
exactly. I don't know whether there's an "aggressive
mutation" in our future, but there was a point
early on in the lockdown when we didn't know
how bad it was going to get.

I'm grateful to my narrator for working through

all those confused feelings on my behalf. I share with him his muddled account of how suspension of disbelief seemed to have broken down. He's confused as well, not quite sure what he feels. I applaud his honesty, although I suspect it's part of the human condition that emotions – fear, dread – don't manifest as a single consistent pressure on the mind.

They don't express themselves too clearly, either. How do you confront an existential threat? How do you look into the abyss without blinking or recoiling? I don't think you do; not directly, anyway. You turn away, you look for the sun, you lie awake at 3am. You become anxious, depressed; you develop one or more physical symptoms. Perhaps also you look for distraction: you don't write the novel but you do read a lot of books; you don't write the screenplay, but wow, you get through some box sets.

You don't see your friends, but you become remarkably proficient at arranging the backgrounds for your Zoom calls. You cook, you put on weight, you find new ways of filling your time. You get distracted. There are birds singing outside my window and the leaves are fluttering in the breeze. I hope my narrator, unreliable though he may be, has managed to distract you for a while at least.

That's it. I've finished. Works as an ending, doesn't it? If I just end it there?

Oh, you want to talk about the deletions. They're not an original idea, you realise that? The trick's been used before.

Okay, maybe you can work this in somewhere.

He writes. That comes through, doesn't it? And he takes himself way too seriously. What he thinks he's doing is just scribbling a journal to clear his mind before he gets on with the serious writing. But it works for him. He's not Writing, capital W, so he can relax into it – which he begins to realise after a while.

The deletions are just – well, first off, he's just scribbling in an abandoned desk diary he's found, so he's going to be crossing out words and correcting himself as he goes along. But after a while he's just slightly composing his thoughts, doing a critique of himself as he goes along. Deleting stuff becomes a technique.

A technique for me, I mean. I used it to show his thought-process as well as his self-presentation. I did say he's an unreliable narrator, didn't I?

I should never have taken that Eng. Lit. degree.

Yeah, I used to get those diaries, back in the day."

Reception

***Escape Mutation* was published** in September 2020 and became a huge worldwide success. William Essex became enormously rich and the two newcomers inhabiting the roles of the narrator and Melusie Evans went on to stellar careers.

The film rights were sold for a truly spectacular amount of money, and the merchandising – in particular the two main action figures and the scaled-down Powder Cottage with the accessory pack – became collectors' items while they were still in the shops – not least because the shops were so rarely open. From the beginning, models changed hands via online auction.

There were rumours of a sequel from the day of *Escape Mutation*'s first publication. William Essex has maintained ever since that the story is complete in itself and no sequel need be written.

However, an email exchange has recently emerged in which William Essex discusses the future of Melusie and Mishka.

According to the emails, which purport to be an exchange between the author and a reader asking whether there's any hope of survival for Mishka, let alone happy ending (William Essex has neither confirmed nor denied the emails' authenticity; the reader's identifying details were erased before the emails were leaked), Mishka and his mother remain on the headland, alive and well and undisturbed, until the boy is (by Melusie's reckoning) twelve.

Then, they leave the cottage and travel inland. They travel at first through a landscape that has completely returned to nature – following the routes of cracked and broken roads overgrown with brambles, bypassing ruined towns, through wild country – until at last they see signs of cultivation. They're cautious at first, and they watch from a distance. There's a farm, and a couple living on the farm, and the couple have … three daughters.

Finally, they make contact. From then on, the emails are all about horse-riding and blackberry picking and (quite quickly) deciding that there's space for all of them to live together in the farmhouse.

In the final email of the series, William Essex reassures his reader that Mishka and his mother won't ever be lonely. He signs off with the line, "They live happily ever after."

About the Author

William Essex lives in Falmouth, Cornwall. He is the author of two novels and one collection of short stories.

Escape Mutation is his first lockdown project.

Lightning Source UK Ltd.
Milton Keynes UK
UKHW011443161221
395754UK00002B/107

9 781909 172975